# DEATH'S H

Bitteroot John redoubl... ...ish Fargo off and get out of there. Their blades locked, separated, locked once more. Both of them strained to their utmost, pivoting for position, their legs braced like sturdy timbers.

It was Fargo who first realized they had strayed even closer to the river. His left foot slid out from under him, and when he straightened to gain solid purchase, there was nothing under him to hold him up. They were at the lip of the bank. Off balance, he teetered.

The buffalo hunter's chance had come. Smirking, he drew back the butcher knife for a final stab. At the same split second a distinct thunk heralded the flight of an arrow. John arched his back, his mouth yawning in a soundless scream. . . .

# THE
# TRAILSMAN
#199

# WYOMING
# WILDCATS

by

**Jon Sharpe**

Ⓞ
A SIGNET BOOK

SIGNET
Published by the Penguin Group
Penguin Putnam Inc., 375 Hudson Street,
New York, New York 10014, U.S.A.
Penguin Books Ltd, 27 Wrights Lane,
London W8 5TZ, England
Penguin Books Australia Ltd,
Ringwood, Victoria, Australia
Penguin Books Canada Ltd, 10 Alcorn Avenue,
Toronto, Ontario, Canada M4V 3B2
Penguin Books (N.Z.) Ltd, 182–190 Wairau Road,
Auckland 10, New Zealand

Penguin Books Ltd, Registered Offices:
Harmondsworth, Middlesex, England

First published by Signet, an imprint of Dutton NAL,
a member of Penguin Putnam Inc.

First Printing, July, 1998
10 9 8 7 6 5 4 3 2 1

The first chapter of this book originally appeared in *Blackgulch Gamble*,
the one hundred ninety-eighth volume in this series.

 REGISTERED TRADEMARK—MARCA REGISTRADA

Printed in the United States of America

# The Trailsman

Beginnings . . . they bend the tree and they mark the man. Skye Fargo was born when he was eighteen. Terror was his midwife, vengeance his first cry. Killing spawned Skye Fargo, ruthless, cold-blooded murder. Out of the acrid smoke of gunpowder still hanging in the air, he rose, cried out a promise never forgotten.

The Trailsman they began to call him all across the West: searcher, scout, hunter, the man who could see where others only looked, his skills for hire but not his soul, the man who lived each day to the fullest, yet trailed each tomorrow. Skye Fargo, the Trailsman, and the seeker who could take the wildness of a land and the wanting of a woman and make them his own.

*1860, the Green River country,*
*where raw lust leads to mayhem and bloodshed. . . .*

# 1

*Someone was stalking him.*

The big man on the pinto stallion was working his way down a steep slope choked with deadfall when the warning screamed in his mind. Skye Fargo could not say exactly how he knew. There had been no crackling of the undergrowth, no snapping of dry twigs. But he knew, just the same, as surely as he did that those stalking him were Indians.

Years of life in the raw had honed the Trailsman's instincts to a razor's edge. Where a city-bred man would see only the deep blue sky and hear only the soft sigh of the breeze and assume all was well, Fargo saw and heard telltale clues he was not alone. The flight of several spooked sparrows, for instance, had been his first inkling of impending danger. The manner in which all the small creatures in his vicinity, all the birds and squirrels and chipmunks, had gone suddenly quiet, was another factor.

Were the Indians peaceable or hostile? That was the big question. Fargo was half a day out from Fort Bridger, in country roamed by both the Shoshones and the Flatheads. Two more friendly tribes would be hard to find. But the Utes also prowled that region from time to time, and of late the Utes had been decidedly unfriendly. Not that Fargo blamed them. With more and more whites pushing into their territory, the Utes were simply protecting what was theirs.

Skirting another tangle of fallen trees, Fargo removed his hat and ran a hand through his dark hair. While doing so, he contrived to swivel his head just enough to scan the ridge he had crossed a couple of minutes ago. Nothing moved up there, but that meant little. If a war party of Utes had decided to ambush him, they would close in like bronzed specters, seldom showing themselves and making no more noise than would real ghosts.

Replacing his hat, Fargo reined to the right, toward a game trail he had spied that wound to a lush valley below. He must hurry without seeming to hurry. For if the Utes should grow aware he had detected them, they would cast stealth to the wind and converge like a pack of ravenous wolves.

His right hand drifted to within easy reach of the Colt nestled snugly in its holster on his hip. In a saddle scabbard under his right leg was a Henry, but he made no move to yank the rifle out just yet. Nor would he resort to the Arkansas toothpick hidden in his boot until it was needed.

It was too bad, Fargo reflected, that he was not in heavy timber. His buckskins would tend to blend into the trees, making it harder for the Utes to keep track of him or fix a bead. He saw the Ovaro prick its ears and look off to the left. Moving just his eyes, he scoured the maze of deadfalls and spotted a blur of motion forty yards away. The brief glimpse had confirmed his hunch. He *was* being hunted, and the hunters were indeed Utes.

Fargo fought down a temptation to apply his spurs. Self-control was called for if he wanted to get out of the tight fix he was in with his scalp intact. To give the Utes the impression he was as green as a newborn babe, he began to hum the tune to a rowdy song popular in saloons and dance halls.

The game trail was barely wide enough for the stallion and pockmarked by the tracks of elk and deer. With the skin at the nape of his neck crawling, Fargo held the pinto to a leisurely gait. He constantly peeked out from under his hat brim at the vegetation on both sides. Chest-high weeds and brush hemmed him in, providing plenty of cover for warriors who might be crouched in waiting.

On his right the grass rustled. Fargo automatically slid his hand to his revolver but checked his draw when a rabbit bounded across the trail. He hoped the Utes had not noticed how edgy he was or they might become suspicious.

The valley floor loomed a stone's throw away. Fargo could not understand why the warriors had not tried to stop him from reaching it. Once he did, he could give the Ovaro its head and literally leave them in the dust. He risked a backward glance to insure they were not slinking up on him. Satisfied, but puzzled, Fargo faced front and lifted the reins. Their mistake was his salvation.

Then a mounted warrior materialized out of a dense stand of cottonwoods sixty feet ahead. Another followed, and another, until there were eight, in all, eight swarthy Utes who spread out as they approached. They walked their horses, in no particular hurry, which told Fargo they were confident they had him trapped. Sure enough, when he glanced over his shoulder again, he discovered another half-dozen warriors had emerged from concealment and were fanning out to block any possible escape.

Fargo had three choices. He could fight, but as yet they had not shown hostile intent and unless they did he would not throw lead at them. He could try to run and get nowhere. Or he could do just what he did, namely, rein up and sit there as calmly as could be while they ringed the pinto.

He was encouraged by the fact they were not painted for war. Among almost all tribes it was customary for men who went on the warpath to paint symbols on their own bodies and on their horses. The symbols, and the meanings attached to them, varied. Common among many tribes was a painted hand, which signified a warrior who had killed an enemy in personal combat. Slash marks were often used to signify the number of coup a man had counted.

Since these Utes and their mounts did not bear the trappings of warfare, Fargo was forced to conclude he had stumbled on a hunting party. On the one hand that was good news. But on the other, he had to question why they had seen fit to sneak up on him and box him in. Holding his right hand in front of his neck with the palm outward and his first and second fingers extended, he raised the hand as high as his head. It was sign language, specifically the sign for "friend."

The Utes halted. They were a somber lot, the frowns they

bestowed on him proof that while they might not be inclined to slit his throat, they were not exactly pleased to run into him either.

A tall Ute had halted his splendid bay in the middle of the game trail, and it was this man who now addressed Fargo in thickly accented English. "We not your friend, white dog." The speaker wore fringed buckskins much like Fargo's own. He carried a lance, and had an ash bow and full quiver slung across his back. A hooked nose dominated his craggy face, and he had a cleft chin, unusual for an Ute. Equally unusual was the wide red headband he wore. Apaches were partial to headbands, as were some of the tribes of the desert country to the southwest, but it was rare to see a plains or mountain Indian wearing one.

"I have done you no harm," Fargo was quick to point out. He did not like how some of the other warriors were fondly fingering weapons. It would not take much to set them off, he reckoned. Better for him if he sheathed his horns and played the part of a perfect innocent. "Why do you treat me as an enemy?"

"You have pale skin," was the tall Ute's reply. "That be reason enough."

"It's not a man's skin that counts but what is in his heart." Fargo picked his words with care. "And my heart has always been open to the red man. I have lived among the Lakota, the Snakes, and others."

The Ute with the headband did not act impressed. Straightening, he gazed beyond Fargo, then at the ridge. "Where be your woman?"

The strange question gave Fargo pause. What did the Utes want with a white woman? While it was fairly common for the Comanches to steal white females, the Utes, to the best of his recollection, had never done so. "I don't have one," he finally admitted.

"All white men have them," the warrior said testily. "I think maybe you speak with two tongues."

Fargo had just been branded a liar. Among Indians, it was an offense worth fighting over, but he dared not provoke the tall Ute or it might set off the rest. Staying as calm as could be, he gestured at his back trail. "Your band has been following me for quite a spell, so you know I speak with a straight tongue."

The warrior's scowl deepened. "I be Red Band," he declared in a way that gave the impression it was a name the Trailsman should be familiar with.

But Fargo had never heard of the man, although it was easy to guess how the Ute came by the handle. "You must be far from the lodges of your people," he said, for lack of anything else to say. At that time of year the Utes were usually found over a week's hard ride to the south.

"Take us to woman."

Fargo's brow knit. What was going on here? Was the Ute playing with him? Maybe deliberately trying to provoke him into going for his gun? It hardly seemed likely. Indians did not generally look for an excuse to kill someone, as whites were prone to do. Curly wolves on the prod liked to taunt their prey into making a grab for a gun so the killers could claim they acted in self-defense. But that hardly applied here. When Indians wanted to kill someone, they just up and did it.

"Take us to woman," Red Band repeated more sternly.

"I've already told you," Fargo said. "I don't have one."

"Take us to other woman. Any woman."

Fargo was beginning to lose his patience but he did not let it show. "Where would I find a female out here in the middle of nowhere?"

"Maybe friend's woman. Maybe settler have wife."

"I don't have any friends in these parts. And I don't know where any settlers might be living. I'm passing through, is all." It was true as far as it went. Fargo really did not know of any acquaintances or homesteaders who might be in the area, but he was not merely passing through. The commander at Fort Bridger had sent for him, and for all he knew, it might have something to do with this band of Utes and their cantankerous leader.

Red Band digested the information a few moments, then leaned over to whisper to the warrior on his right. They talked a bit, then Red Band squared his broad shoulders and declared, "You come with us. Find us woman."

There was only so much a man could take. Fargo casually shifted so his right hand was closer to the Colt, and replied, "I'm not going anywhere with you. If you want a woman so damn much, go to your village and take yourself a wife."

"I want white woman."

"Too bad," Fargo said, and slapped his legs against the Ovaro. The stallion reacted superbly, bounding forward and breaking into a gallop. They were on the Utes so quickly that none of the warriors had time to unleash a shaft or hurl a lance. Fargo flashed between Red Band and one of the others. Red Band grabbed for him but Fargo rammed a hand against the Ute's chest and sent Red Band toppling. In another instant he was past the line and racing westward, bent low over the saddle to make as small a target of himself as he could.

Yips and war whoops rent the air. The warriors were in full pursuit, except for two who were helping their leader.

Fargo braced for a flurry of arrows but no shafts were loosed. Apparently the Utes wanted him alive, not dead. That was small consolation since their mounts appeared to be sturdy and fleet. Eluding them would not be easy. But Fargo had every confidence in the Ovaro. The pinto had saved their hides on more occasions than he could count.

With a flick of the reins Fargo sent the stallion pounding down onto the valley floor and off across it through knee-high grass. Thunder rumbled in their wake, the hammering of eleven sets of heavy hooves. Red Band and the two others were further back, Red Band having just mounted to give chase.

Fargo jammed his hat low so it would not be blown off. He had a twenty-yard lead but that was nowhere near enough. Angling toward verdant woodland that fringed the valley to the north, he rode flat out. The swish of the grass against the stallion's legs was nearly drowned out by the yells and screeches of the incensed Utes. Right away it became obvious that three of them were going to give him the most trouble. The trio had pulled ahead of the pack and were more than holding their own. One was on a roan, the other two rode sorrels.

It occurred to Fargo to pull out his rifle and shoot their horses out from under them. That is what most any other frontiersman would have done. But Fargo was not one of those who killed animals without cause. He'd met men who did, men who shot things for the hell of it, not because they were hungry or needed a hide or even because they were after trophy game. Fargo never shot anyone or anything unless it was justified.

A meandering stream appeared out of the grass, a ribbon of water barely deeper than the Ovaro's knees. Fargo flew across, water spraying every which way. On the other side was a low bank and he started up it only to suddenly feel the stallion slip and tilt wildly to the left. A glance explained why. The lower portion of the bank had crumpled under the Ovaro's weight, and now the pinto's hooves were churning at slippery dank earth instead of solid ground.

A cry of triumph was voiced by the nearest Ute, a burly warrior whose roan was the swiftest animal in the band. He closed in rapidly, narrowing the gap to fifteen yards, to ten. In his left hand he held a war club which he raised overhead.

The Ovaro gave a prodigious lunge upward and cleared the bank. Fargo did not look back again until he was almost to the tree line. The Ute on the roan was a dozen yards off, the pair on sorrels twice that. The rest of the band had lost so much distance they no longer posed a threat.

Into the forest Fargo streaked. Weaving and winding among the pines and firs, he pushed the stallion as hard as he dared. What with logs and ruts and other obstacles popping up in the blink of an eye, he had to be fully alert every single second. A single misstep might be disastrous.

For long minutes the race went on, Fargo never able to gain more than a few extra yards. The three Utes clung to him like glue, particularly the warrior on the roan, who was as fine a horseman as Fargo had ever seen. Soon it became obvious that in order to shake them Fargo must resort to something more drastic.

But what? Shooting one would arouse bloodlust in the whole band. They would not rest until they had tracked him down and had their revenge. Even if he managed to elude them, they would return to their people and tell what had happened. Word would spread from their village to all the others, and before too long the whole tribe would be on the lookout for him. Every time he crossed their territory in the future, he would be taking his life in his hands.

There had to be a way to escape without spilling blood. But try as Fargo might, he could not think of how to accomplish it. He was still racking his brain when the trees thinned at the base of a hill. He started up without bothering to look closely. Too late, he saw the talus that littered the slope from top to bottom. Loose rocks and dirts spewed out from under the Ovaro as the stallion churned its legs to stay upright.

"Damn!" Fargo fumed at his own carelessness. He had blundered at the worst possible moment.

The pinto had to slow down or it would fall. Fargo picked his way with supreme care, climbing slowly and chafing at the delay, slanting to the left rather than going straight up. A fierce whoop reminded him of the Ute on the roan.

The warrior had shot from the woods, seen the pinto struggling, and hurtled to intercept it before it could get any higher. But the same talus that had nearly upended the Ovaro now had the same effect on the roan. Stones and gravel rained down from under its flailing hooves. It slipped and slid, lurching from side to side as if drunk.

Trying to ride on talus was like trying to ride on thick, slick ice. The debris that sometimes accumulated was as unstable as a house built of cards. It did not take much to send the whole mass cascading downward in a violent rocky avalanche. Seasoned riders knew to avoid talus as they would coiled rattlers.

Fargo continued to climb. Going back down would be twice as hard, and put him in the hands of the Utes. Already the pair on sorrels had arrived and were gingerly moving toward him. The warrior on the roan steadied his animal, then advanced, taking his sweet time.

The Ovaro had done this before. It knew to place each leg

down as lightly as if treading on egg shells. All Fargo had to do was avoid gaps and areas he deemed especially unsafe. Every now and then stones would roll out from under them, but never enough to cause the pinto to slip. Time dragged. The hot sun baked the talus, causing rippling waves of heat to rise from the rocks and boulders. By the time Fargo was halfway to the top, he was caked with sweat.

In a flurry of crackling brush the remainder of the band reached the hill. Red Band pushed to the front and glared. "Come back!" he hollered. "I want woman!"

Fargo had never met anyone so female-hungry in all his born days. And why it had to be a white woman, he had no idea. Maybe Red Band had a personal hankering, like the mountain men and trappers Fargo had known who favored Indian women. He pressed on, paying no heed when Red Band and the rest began to scale the hill.

The Ute on the roan was doing remarkably well. The roan was like a mountain goat, moving agilely for a horse its size. It soon made up the ground it had lost. A wicked gleam lit the warrior's eyes and he eagerly fingered his war club. Presently he would be close enough to throw it, which posed a very real threat.

Fargo took a gamble. He was twenty feet below a flat crest on which a few trees stood. The talus was thinner higher up, less slippery but still treacherous. Urging the Ovaro briskly on, he sought the firmest footing, veering to avoid a cleft that would pitch them both down the hill. The Ute on the roan, venting a yelp of frustration, goaded the roan to catch up.

The Ovaro slipped, recovered its balance, and forged upward. Fargo was almost to the rim when he saw a long log to his right. A final lash of the reins, and he reached safety. Immediately vaulting from the saddle, he dashed to the log, squatted, and pushed. It would not budge. He threw his shoulder against it and it started to slide, then wedged fast. Meanwhile, the Utes steadily drew nearer. The man on the roan was fifteen feet below, the roan floundering on a patch of pebbles and dirt.

Flinging himself onto his back, Fargo wedged both of his

boots against the dead pine, bunched the muscles in his stomach and legs, and heaved outward with all his might. The log shook and rolled but only a couple of inches. Gritting his teeth, he tried again. He could hear the roan clattering closer, ever closer. The sneering visage of the warrior hove into view. In another few moments the Ute would spring.

Exerting every sinew that packed his powerful frame, Fargo drove his legs against the log. It tilted, shifted, and broke free. Gaining speed, it rolled against the roan, and the horse panicked. Nickering and kicking, the animal tried to back away but in its haste it stepped on a wide flat rock that shot off down the slope. The Ute hauled on the reins in vain. Squealing in fear, the roan lost its footing, and horse and rider tumbled.

The log resumed rolling, gaining speed as it traveled, dislodging talus that flowed in its wake. As more and more boulders and rocks were dislodged, the flow became a torrent. In a twinkling the entire slope seemed to be on the move, sweeping toward the startled Utes.

Red Band shouted and motioned for his warriors to flee, but only a few at the very bottom had any hope of evading the avalanche. Most were caught in the act of turning. Horses squealed in fright, men bellowed in fury. Swept into the swirling current of stone and earth, they were helpless to resist. One man leaped off his mount and tried to reach the side of the hill on foot before the talus reached him. He failed.

Fargo rose and forked leather. It would take the Utes a while to catch their horses and come after him. By then he would be long gone. He rose in the stirrups for a last look and saw Red Band go down. As the Ute was bowled over, he glanced up and shook a fist in impotent outrage. Fargo smiled.

In a rattling deluge the rockslide roiled to the base of the hill and spilled out over the grass. Warriors and horses were strewn about like chaff in the wind. None showed evidence of being seriously hurt, although one horse limped when it stood and one of the Utes cradled an arm that was bent at an unnatural angle.

Turning westward, Fargo left them eating dust. As soon as they were out of sight he shut the incident from his mind. It was just one of many similar events that were part and parcel of life in the wilderness. Besides, he mused, it was highly doubtful he would ever run into Red Band again.

The summer's day was young yet, the heat of late morning soon to be eclipsed by a hotter afternoon. Fargo loosened his bandanna and pushed his hat back. Provided there were no other interruptions, he should reach Fort Bridger by nightfall.

Built on the left bank of Black's Fork of the Green River, the fort had originally been a trading post built by the famed mountain man, Jim Bridger. Old Jim and the Mormons who settled to the west of him in Utah never had gotten along, and eight years ago the Mormons had driven Bridger out, claiming he was too friendly with the Indians. Not true! Old Jim told the government. He complained that the Mormons wanted his lucrative trading post and the land it sat on for themselves. And he might have been right.

Before the government got around to doing anything about it, the Mormons rose up in arms. The Utah War, folks called it. Started because Mormon men were fond of having as many wives as an Arab sheik, and the government kept telling them, "Only one. Only one." The Army marched on Utah. So out of sheer spite, the Mormons burned the post to the ground.

Old Jim got back at them, though. He volunteered to guide the federal troops to Salt Lake City. Later, he leased the site of his trading post to the military, and Fort Bridger was erected.

Nowadays the post was a vital link in the chain of forts that crisscrossed the frontier. It was a major supply depot for troops farther west. It helped to guard the Overland Trail. Last of all, but most important, it helped to keep the Utes in line.

Fargo had been there before, and not much had changed since his last visit. From a spine of land he surveyed the broad green valley in which it was located. The Green River was aptly named. Along its fertile banks many of the old-time rendezvous were held by the hardy beaver trappers who once roamed the mountains in search of prime peltries. Above the high walls of the fort fluttered a flag. To the northwest a dozen lodges had been set up by Indians who had ventured to the post to trade.

No homesteads were in evidence, and for that Fargo was grateful. In his estimation, far too many settlers had flocked westward in recent years. Already cabins and sod houses dotted the landscape from Texas clear to Canada. Denver had recently been incorporated as a *city*, and other towns in the central Rockies were flourishing. For someone who loved the pristine wilds as much as Fargo did, the influx of Easterners was a sorry state of affairs.

The gates were wide open. Bored sentries lounged on either side, neither giving Fargo more than a casual scrutiny as he entered. Tired troops drilled on the parade ground. In front of the sutler's half a dozen Shoshones were haggling over furs they had brought in.

Fargo made straight for the headquarters building. In front of it two small covered wagons were parked. As he swung around the tongue of the first one to reach a hitching post, a pair of slender figures blundered directly into his path and he had to haul on the reins to keep from colliding with them.

"Watch where you're going!" the tall one bawled.

"Don't you have eyes?" snapped the other.

They were women. The tallest was a shapely brunette whose piercing green eyes shone with vitality. Her companion was a petite but amply endowed blonde whose blue eyes were as icy as the craggy heights of Long's Peak. Finding two such luscious females at the post was surprising enough. But even more shocking was to see them both in men's clothes, pants and flannel shirts and all.

"Look at him, Diane." The brunette sniffed.

"Sitting there gaping like the dumb brute he is," responded the other. "How typical of a man, Hester."

Fargo was too flabbergasted to comment.

Just then a man in uniform stepped from the headquarters building, saw him, and came over, offering a hand. "Let me guess. You must be the scout we sent for, the Trailsman. The dispatch said you would be riding a big pinto stallion. I'm Major Edward Canby, tenth U.S. Infantry, the one who sent for you. It's an honor, sir, to make your acquaintance."

"Major," Fargo said, tearing his gaze from the two lovelies.

"They told me at Fort Laramie that I had to get here as quickly as I could. What's the trouble?"

Major Canby blinked. "Why, none whatsoever. Didn't they tell you why you were needed?" He pointed at the women. "We'd like you to guide these two ladies into Indian country."

# 2

To say Skye Fargo was angry would be an understatement. He had ridden like the very devil to reach Fort Bridger in as short a time as he could, pushing the poor Ovaro to its limit. Both of them had gone without much food and little sleep. And as if all that were not bad enough, there had been the clash with the Utes. Hardship, hunger, hostiles, he had endured them all, and for what? Because a couple of uppity ladies needed someone to do what any halfway competent frontiersman could handle! "I have half a mind to get down and punch you in the mouth, Major," he said bitterly.

Canby recoiled as if he *had* been struck. "What on earth for?"

Stabbing a finger at the three rugged buckskin-clad figures lounging near the barracks, Fargo said, "Unless I miss my guess, those men are on the army's payroll. Why send for me when you have plenty of your own scouts?"

Major Canby rather self-consciously gestured at the two women. "It wasn't my idea, Mr. Fargo, I assure you. Our distinguished guests insisted on the best man for the job, and no one has a more justly deserved reputation than you do."

Fargo swung toward the pair, glowering as if he were about to pounce. The brunette stiffened but the blonde stood there as calm as you please. "So this harebrained idea was yours?" he snapped.

Hester, the brunette, regained her composure and responded, "Now see here. I don't know where you get off talking to us like this." She poked a thumb at Canby. "Isn't it insubordination for a lowly scout to speak so rudely to his commanding officer? Why, I should think they would have you flogged for violating army rules of conduct."

"In the first place, lady," Fargo growled, "I'm not *in* the army. I help them out from time to time, but I'm not an enlisted man. So I can do as I damn well please." He leaned on the saddle horn. "In the second place, if you used that pretty head of yours for something other than a hat rack now and then, you'd see how much trouble you've put me through. And all for nothing."

The blonde, Diane, arched a delicate eyebrow. "What exactly does that cryptic comment portend?" she demanded.

"Portend?" Fargo repeated. He hadn't known the twosome two minutes, and already he had them pegged as snotty Easterners who liked to throw around highfalutin words to show they were better than everyone else. "I'll make this as clear as I can," he said, speaking as slowly and clearly as an adult would to a wayward child. "It will be a cold day in hell before I guide the two of you anywhere. Savvy?"

Hester's cheeks turned scarlet. "Well, I never! Such crude talk, and in the presence of perfect ladies."

"It's obvious he's no gentleman," Diane agreed. "Ruffians like this have no conception of how to treat women."

It galled Fargo how they talked about him as if he were not even there. He had half a mind to dump them both in the nearest horse trough. Instead, wheeling the Ovaro, he said to the major, "I'll stay the night, if you have no objection."

"None at all. Help yourself to feed for your animal," Canby said, then moved closer. "Listen, I'm truly sorry about this misunderstanding. I was only following orders when I sent for you." He bobbed his chin at the women. "General Weaver instructed me to do whatever they want, and they insisted you work for them."

"Over my dead body," Fargo said loudly so the women could not help overhearing. Thinking that was that, he rode to the stable. An overworked young private dressed in a baggy stable frock and trousers promised to give the stallion plenty of grain and see that the pinto had a stall all to itself. In appreciation, Fargo slipped him a silver dollar.

"Gee, thanks, mister." The trooper beamed, admiring the coin. "It's been a coon's age since I had me one of these."

"Hold on to it," Fargo advised. Army pay was notoriously low. More often than not, it was also late in arriving. Not a day or two late, but a whole week or more, sometimes an entire month. When the soldiers finally did get the money due, they had bills to pay at the sutler's, fines to pay for infractions, money to send home to loved ones, or else they made the mistake of sitting in on a card game. It was not uncommon for soldiers to be flat broke one day after the paymaster dispersed their funds.

With the Henry under one arm and his saddlebags thrown over the opposite shoulder, Fargo strolled out into the bright sunlight. A meal was in order. He would eat until he was fit to burst, then find himself a quiet spot and curl up for a nice long sleep. He paid no attention to the two winsome figures who barred his way and tried to go around them, but he should have known it would not be that easy.

"We'd like a word with you," the blonde said as if she were a queen addressing a lowly subject. She gripped his sleeve.

"No."

The brunette sniffed in annoyance. "Honestly, you are one of the rudest men I've ever met. You'll hear us out whether you want to or not."

"Care to bet?" Fargo jerked his arm free and kept on going but the persistent pair trailed along.

"Now listen here," the blonde declared. "I happen to be Diane Marsten. Professor Marsten, to you, temporarily on attached service to the Corps of Topographical Engineers."

Fargo had heard of the corps. Since 1853 it had been engaged in mapping the vast uncharted territory that stretched from the mighty Mississippi to the sandy shores of the pounding Pacific. Word had it that by the time the engineers were done, every square foot of wilderness would have been covered. Fargo doubted that very much, but it troubled him just the same. The survey was another troubling harbinger of things to come, a sign that sooner rather than later hordes of

24

settlers would pour into the West, spoiling forever the raw un-tamed land he called home.

"I'm Professor Hester Williams," the brunette revealed. "We were asked to head this expedition because of our exper-tise in related fields, and because the army has a shortage of qualified engineers of its own."

Fargo could not care less. "Keep your eyes skinned for the Blackfeet and the Piegans. They hate whites." He walked faster to lose them but this time it was Hester who snagged some of the whangs on his sleeve.

"Hold on. Can't you be civil for a minute and hear us out?"

"Yes," added Diane. "We figure it's the least you can do."

"You figured wrong," Fargo bluntly replied, recollecting what they had called him earlier. "I'm a dumb brute, remem-ber? And brutes don't know how to be polite." He touched the brim of his hat in parting and ambled toward the sutler's, leav-ing them to stew. The place was pleasantly cool and well stocked for a small frontier fort. Dry goods were on one side, perishables on the other. A pickle barrel accounted for a sour tangy scent. A few soldiers were wistfully browsing, while the Shoshones who had brought pelts to trade were picking through a pile of blankets.

At the counter stood a beefy man whose features lit in a genuinely friendly smile. "What can I do for you, stranger?"

"Any chance of getting a hot meal?" Fargo asked.

"Sorry. There's never any demand. The troops all eat free at the mess, so why should they pay for food?" The sutler turned to a shelf. "But I have something here you might like. Just came in last week." Rising onto his toes, he retrieved a large can. "The latest thing. So tasty, you'll swear they were plucked fresh this morning." He lowered his voice as if to con-fide a secret. "To tell the truth, the damn things are addicting. I've eaten three whole cans myself. At the rate I'm going, I won't make a penny of profit off them."

"Off what?"

"Peaches," the sutler disclosed, displaying the bright label. "In sweet syrup as thick as molasses. Guaranteed to be deli-cious or your money back. So help me."

Other than coffee, Fargo seldom ate anything from cans. Canned goods were expensive and much too heavy to lug around on long treks. It was less costly and much easier to simply live off the land, as the Indians did. But he accepted it and examined a gaudily painted peach below the words, "FROM THE GARDEN OF EDEN TO YOUR MOUTH."

"I thought patent medicine salesmen were bad," he muttered.

The sutler chuckled. "That ain't the half of it. You should see some of the literature I get, advertising goods they want me to sell. Why, the other day I got in a pamphlet for a new-fangled type of food called the potato chip. They claim it's as thin as a whisker and crunchy like hard candy. Can you imagine?"

Fargo absently nodded and paid. Venturing outdoors, he sat on the edge of the porch, slid the Arkansas toothpick from its sheath, and proceeded to open the can by gouging holes along the rim and prying until the metal came loose. Inside, peach halves floated in gooey syrup. He speared one and took a bite.

"We're not done talking to you."

Not bothering to look up, Fargo said with his mouth full, "Go pester somebody else."

"Be quiet and listen," Diane Marsten said. "We're sure that once you understand why we sent for you, you'll stop behaving so childishly and agree to our proposal."

"That's right," Hester Williams agreed. "Even someone with your limited intellect should be able to grasp the importance of our task. Surely you've heard that the railroad will be coming through this area one day?" She did not wait for him to answer. "When it does, it will bring progress and prosperity to everyone. Towns and cities will spring up all across this great country of ours."

Fargo munched on the juicy peach and paid her no heed. Or tried to. For a professor, she had a lilting musical voice that would do justice to a dance hall dove. Nor did it help that her more than ample bosom thrust against the fabric of her shirt as if seeking to rip through the material.

Diane Marsten was studying him. "You're not listening, are

you? You honestly don't care about the future of our magnificent nation, do you?" She shook her head in disgust. "Haven't you heard about Manifest Destiny? About the duty we have to overspread the continent allotted by Providence for the free development of our yearly multiplying millions?"

Fargo paused in the act of taking another bite and looked at her.

"What's the matter?" Diane said. "Why are you staring at me like that?"

"You must read dictionaries for fun."

"What if I do?" the blonde shot back. "What do you do for entertainment? Collect lice out of your hair?"

Both women laughed merrily. Fargo finished the peach, tilted the can to his lips, and took a long, noisy sip. He deliberately smacked his lips and grunted like an overfed bear. Lancing the tip of the throwing knife into another piece, he ate with relish, slurping like a four-year-old.

"How barbaric," Hester said. "Didn't anyone ever teach you manners?"

Fargo slurped louder, sucking part of the peach into his mouth. When some syrup oozed onto his fingers, he licked them clean, then sucked loudly on the end of each.

"I can't stand to watch this crude display," Hester declared. "I feel positively queasy." She started to leave.

"Don't go," Diane Marsten said. "He's doing it on purpose."

"What?"

"Mr. Fargo is making a spectacle of himself at our expense. He thinks that by behaving so abominably, we'll leave him in peace." A hint of a grin cracked the blonde's icy demeanor. "I suspect he is more intelligent than we have given him credit for being. Perhaps we should stop badgering him and present our case."

The brunette was dubious but she motioned at the wagons and said, "See those, Mr. Fargo? They're loaded with valuable equipment worth thousands of dollars. Theodolites, tripods, compasses, telescopes, you name it, we've spared no expense in obtaining the very best that money can buy. Naturally, we do not want anything to happen to it."

Diane Marsten broke in when Hester paused for breath. "No matter what you might think of us, we're not idiots. We're aware of the dangers that lurk in the wild, and we were assured a competent guide could help steer us clear of them. Ergo, we requested the very best scout there is."

"I'm still not interested," Fargo said.

"Every man has his price," Hester Williams stated. "Name yours, and if it's within reason, we'll pay it."

"The government is keen to have the survey completed," Diane said. "Without it, the railroad will be delayed."

Despite himself, Fargo was growing interested. It helped that both women were so attractive. Hester had a cute button of a nose, pouty full lips, and pert breasts that jiggled when she moved. Diane was molded more like the classical beauties found in paintings that hung over every bar in every saloon on the frontier. Most of those paintings were cheap reproductions but they captured the grace and bloom of their subjects quite well. "What area do you intend to survey?"

Diane winked at Hester. "North along the Green River, then northeast to the Wind River Range. It shouldn't take more than a few weeks. All you have to do is guide us. We've hired a fellow called Bitterroot John to be our cook and do camp chores. The fourth member of our party, Clark Upton, from the St. Louis Academy of Science, will handle the heavy equipment."

Fargo had to admit that it sounded like an easy way to make some poker money. "Two hundred dollars, in advance."

Hester had said he could name his price, but now she acted as if he had asked for a king's ransom. "Two hundred? We're only paying Bitterroot John fifty. And Clark is along merely to study the fauna and flora. We don't have to pay him a cent."

"Then let him guide you." Fargo devoted himself to the peaches while they retreated and bickered in whispers. He caught snatches of their spirited conversation. Hester did not want to pay him more than seventy-five, but Diane pointed out that it would be money well spent if he saved them time and inconvenience. He was almost to the bottom of the can when their shadows fell across him again.

"Very well," Hester said reluctantly. "Two hundred it is. But you had better be worth it. I must account to the government for every dollar we spend, and they don't take kindly to squandering funds."

"Since when?" Fargo quipped, and downed the last of the syrup by upending the can. Rising, he stretched and stifled a yawn. "How soon do you want to leave?"

"Tomorrow morning would be ideal," Diane said. "We're all packed and the wagons are set to roll. They have been for over a week. Frankly, I'm tired of being cooped up at this post. I'd like to get out and see some of the countryside." She stretched, too, and in doing so her breasts strained against her shirt in ripe, luscious outline.

Fargo's throat went unaccountably dry. He envisioned tweaking her hard nipple with his tongue and felt stirrings below his waist. "I'll check your supplies and see if anything is missing." Setting the empty can on a bench, he scooped up the Henry and his saddlebags and headed for the wagons. The two professors fell into step beside him. Hester wore a tantalizing perfume that tingled his nostrils. Diane had a more subtle scent, an earthy, musky aroma that brought to mind canopy beds and down quilts.

The first wagon contained the survey equipment. Four theodolites were strapped down tight in order to prevent them from being jostled and damaged. "We brought along a couple of spares as a prudent precaution," Hester mentioned.

In the second wagon were the supplies. There was a portable stove, a small table, and folding stools, and pots and pans. Plates and cups, silverware, even lacy napkins had been packed. Lanterns hung from hooks. Coffee, cheese, jerked meat, and pickled fish were in one corner. In another were barrels brimming with sugar, flour, and molasses. Fargo guessed they had enough food to last six months.

"Is there anything we've forgotten?" Diane asked as he climbed down.

"I didn't see any guns."

Hester scrunched up her face as if he had suggested they tote along a ton of buffalo droppings. "I don't like firearms, Mr. Fargo. They are the last resort of the primitive."

"Tell that to a Piegan about to lift your hair," Fargo said. "You'll need a rifle and a revolver for each member of your survey crew plus a hundred rounds of ammunition each."

"Four hundred rounds!?" Hester exclaimed. "What are you planning to do? Wage war?"

"It's better to have ammo to spare than to not have any when you need it most," Fargo noted.

The brunette opened her mouth to object but Diane silenced her with a wave. "We'll do as Mr. Fargo requests. He knows best."

"But I've never shot a firearm in my life," Hester protested. "I doubt I could ever hit anything even if I had to. So why don't we just buy some for the rest of you and let it go at that?"

"I'll give you lessons," Fargo said, stepping onto the porch. "Come on. Let's see what we have to pick from."

The sutler stocked plenty of guns. Fargo hoped to find several Henry rifles like his own, but the Henry was new to the frontier and few were available anywhere. The sutler had sold his last one a couple of months ago. That was unfortunate. Able to hold fifteen shots in a tubular magazine, the .44-caliber Henry was far superior to anything else on the market. It did not have the range of a Big Fifty, or the sheer stopping power of a 45-70, but it could fire thirty shots a minute, a feat no other rifle could duplicate.

The sutler did have half a dozen Sharps but Fargo did not select any of them. Having used one for quite a spell before he switched to the Henry, he knew firsthand the Sharps packed too much of a wallop for the women. That, and the Sharps was a single-shot weapon. Each big cartridge had to be inserted by working the trigger guard, which acted much the same as the Henry's lever. It was a slow process. He had been adept at it, yet he never was able to get off more than five or six shots in a minute's time.

That left Fargo with a choice of several old flintlocks or

some Spencers. He chose the latter. Like the Henry, the Spencer was a repeating rifle. It differed in that the rounds were ejected by pumping the trigger guard, and it held only seven rounds in a tubular magazine inserted into the stock.

Fargo picked one for each member of the survey expedition. Next he turned to a display case of six-guns. Here he had a wider selection to choose from. The sutler had Colts, of course, including the cumbersome Walker, the more recent army and navy models, and others. There were also Remingtons, Smith & Wessons, Allen & Wheelocks, Whitneys, and a revolver manufactured by the Massachusetts Arms Company.

Fargo examined every one, checking their craftsmanship, testing their balance, and noting their calibers. He decided on two .36-caliber Whitneys for the women and a pair of Colt Navies for the cook and the man from the St. Louis Academy of Science. The sutler was more than happy to fill the order. "Thanks to these ladies," he commented at one point, "I've sold more in the past week than I have in the past year."

The two professors had little to say. Diane Marsten held a Spencer at Fargo's request to insure it was not too heavy for her to handle. But Hester Williams refused to so much as touch one. "I told you. I want nothing to do with guns," she insisted.

Fargo bought Green River knives for both of them and told them to wear the knives at all times once they were on the trail. Diane strapped hers on then and there but Hester inspected hers a moment, sniffed in disdain, and dropped it on the counter.

"You have something against knives, too?" Fargo asked.

"I despise all weapons of war. Humankind would be much better off if they were abolished from use."

Fargo had heard about people like her but had never run into one before. People who viewed the world through the rosy quartz prism of their own misguided beliefs. It was commendable that they disliked seeing bloodshed, but violence was a common occurrence in the wilderness. In life, for that matter. Trying to ignore it would not make it go away. He hefted the hilt of the Green River blade. "This has a hundred uses other than to kill."

"It's sharp, isn't it?" Hester said indignantly.

Fargo did not waste his breath arguing. Stupidity was its own worst enemy. Nothing he could say would make her come to her senses. Only experience could do that, experience she would hopefully live through.

At that juncture into the store walked a dapper man in a clean suit and a derby hat. Middle-aged and graying at the temples, he doffed his hat to the women, then faced the Trailsman. "Skye Fargo, I presume? Greetings to you, sir. Major Canby just informed me that you had arrived. Now we can finally get under way." His neatly manicured hand was extended. "I'm Professor Clark Upton. Perhaps Professor Marsten or Professor Williams told you about me?"

Fargo nodded as he shook. Upton's grip was surprisingly strong for a city-bred fellow, his gaze open and frank. Fargo liked him on the spot. "We leave at first light."

"Excellent, simply excellent!" Upton declared. "To be in the field again! I can hardly wait." He coughed self-consciously, then said, "You must excuse my enthusiasm, sir. You see, I don't get out into the wild nearly as often as I should. Most of my time is spent teaching. Nine months of the year I sit behind a desk trying to impart a smidgen of knowledge to adolescent know-it-alls who have no interest whatsoever in anything except the opposite gender."

"Professor!" Hester Williams said, scandalized. "Please. There are women present."

"It's true and you know it." Upton held his ground. "Sex is all college-aged men and women think about. It's all I thought about when I was twenty. Were you any different?"

Hester imitated a beet and sputtered in moral outrage. "My personal life is none of your business, thank you very much. And whether I think about—*that*—is certainly not a fit topic for public discussion." Spinning, she stomped out in a huff, her long hair swirling about her slender shoulders, her slim hips swaying enticingly with each stride.

"As Shakespeare might put it, Methinks the wench doth protest too much," Clark Upton said. "Ah, well. More's the pity. If she were more hot-blooded, it would make our little jaunt into the mountains much more interesting."

Diane Marsten, Fargo noticed, had not blushed or so much as batted an eye. Folding her arms, she regarded Upton with amusement more than anything else. "Clark, you know how she is. Why set her off? Now I'll have to go and smooth her ruffled feathers or she'll be unbearable the whole trip."

"Oh really, Diane," Upton said. "Can I help it if your friend is as frigid as an iceberg? Mark my words. If she doesn't mend her ways and join the human race, she'll end her days as a wretched spinster wallowing in misery."

"Maybe so," Diane said, "but that doesn't let you off the hook. You promised me, Clark. You gave me your word before we left St. Louis that you would behave. Are you going back on it now?"

"No, no. Never, dear heart." Upton took her hand in his and with a flourish and a bow, kissed her knuckles. "Excuse my atrocious manners. From this moment on I shall be a paragon of virtue and gentlemanly behavior."

Laughing, Diane Marsten smacked his shoulder. "Go on, you lecher. Get out of here. Go ogle those Indian maidens you've been admiring all morning before I forget myself and hit you with a frying pan."

Upton grinned at Fargo, and departed.

"He's one of my best friends," Diane explained. "You'd never guess to look at him that he has degrees in both botany and zoology. He should have a third, in womanizing. His favorite pastime is to visit a certain house of ill repute and spend days there in utter debauchery."

Fargo idly wondered why it was that those with a college education always talked as if they were living books. He shifted to tell the sutler to put the guns in the supply wagon when suddenly two men tramped through the doorway, both burly bears in buckskins. In the lead was a grimy hulk with a greasy beard and oily hair and hands as big as cooking pots. Planting himself, the man raked Fargo from head to toe in critical contempt.

"So you're the son of a bitch who thinks he's goin' to lead the survey outfit. Well, guess what, mister? You're wrong."

# 3

Skye Fargo recollected seeing the pair before, lounging near the barracks. They were army scouts, men who made their living much as he did, hard men tempered by a hard life. Men who were quick with a knife or a gun. Men who, like him, did not appreciate having their toes stepped on.

Fargo gave them no warning of what he was going to do. He did not threaten or bluff. He did not try to talk his way out of the situation. His right fist streaked up and out and caught the first scout just above his greasy beard, full on the mouth. The impact jolted the man backward into the second one and both tumbled against the jamb and would have fallen if the second scout had not braced himself.

Spitting blood and swearing, the first man heaved upright, balled his huge paws, and bore down on Fargo like a bull buffalo gone amok. "Lay a hand on me, will you? No one does that and gets away with it!"

The sutler moved toward the end of the counter, yelling, "See here! That's enough out of you, Groff. I won't have you acting up in my place, you hear?"

Groff stalked forward, his right arm cocked. Scarlet drops flecked his beard and cheek. He was too mad to listen, too mad to stop. Bellowing, he threw his whole weight into a roundhouse right that would have caved in Skye Fargo's teeth if it had landed.

Fargo ducked, then delivered an uppercut that rocked Groff on his heels. Following through with a series of swift jabs, Fargo drove the scout toward the doorway. Groff tried to block the jabs but he was too ponderous, a bruiser not a skilled fighter, a brawler who relied on sheer strength to overpower his foes. Fargo countered a looping left, retaliated with a jarring hook to the body, and brought Groff crashing to the floor with a blistering right to the jaw.

"Damn you!" the second man cried, and waded in to take up where Groff had left off.

"Belcher! No!" the sutler shouted, to no avail.

Belcher was slightly smaller and faster than his partner, and he knew enough to hold his fists in a boxing posture and not to overextend himself as Groff had done. Flicking one punch after another, he battered at Fargo's guard, trying to land a solid blow. Fargo was not about to let him. Twisting and pivoting, he evaded most of Belcher's swings while scoring with a few of his own.

It made Belcher angry and he grew reckless. Snorting like a black bear, Belcher flung himself forward and grabbed Fargo's left wrist. He tried to grasp the right one but Fargo yanked it back, rotated on the balls of his feet, and drove his fist into the pit of Belcher's gut. The scout doubled over, wheezing like a bellows.

Sweeping a knee up, Fargo slammed it into Belcher's face. The man went down like a pole ox. Fargo straightened to catch his breath but he was denied the opportunity. Groff was back on his feet, and with an inarticulate roar he charged, lowering a shoulder to bowl Fargo over.

Sidestepping, Fargo clipped Groff on the back of the head. He spun to confront Groff as the man whirled to attack again. Without warning, arms clamped onto his from behind, and held fast. Belcher had recovered much sooner than Fargo had anticipated.

Groff smiled a sadistic smile and slowly advanced. "Hold him good and tight, pard," he said. "I want to beat him silly before I stave in his ribs."

"Take your time," Belcher said. "He's not gettin' loose."

The scout was wrong. Fargo snapped his head back, into Belcher's nose, and heard a distinct crunch. Simultaneously, he levered his foot to the rear, up into Belcher's groin. A strangled grunt was proof he had connected. Groff sprang to his friend's aid, but Fargo tucked at the waist and whipped around, in effect flinging Belcher into Groff. The two men landed in a tangle of limbs.

The sutler was beside himself. Prancing and dancing like someone with ants in his britches, he flapped his arms and bawled, "Enough! Enough! Stop it before you damage my merchandise!"

Groff and Belcher had cotton in their ears. In unison they surged upright and came toward Fargo, shoulder to shoulder this time, relying on craftiness rather than brute force. "You hit the bastard high, I'll go low," Belcher said.

Fargo did not wait for them to reach him. Taking a bound, he leaped into the air, his right boot lashing out against Groff's chest. Groff staggered but did not go down. And in that instant when Fargo was off his feet and off balance, Belcher seized the chance and rammed into him, Belcher's shoulder striking him across the hip. Fargo desperately tried to straighten but it was a lost cause. He crashed onto his back. Instantly, the pair were on him like wolves on a stricken elk.

Fargo thrust a boot into Belcher's midsection and knocked the scout sideways. Groff smashed down on top of him, though, and succeeded in pinning his left arm. Lancing a knee into Groff's side, Fargo wrenched to the right and pushed. He dislodged Groff, but took a boot in the back from Belcher. Wincing at the agony, he scrambled away to gain room to move. They were not about to let him. Converging, both scouts rained punches. It was all Fargo could do to ward off some of them. His ear stung, his cheek was bruised, his jaw absorbed a blow that would have rendered most men unconscious

Rolling onto his stomach, Fargo let his back take more abuse while he coiled his legs and tensed his arms. Suddenly hurtling upward, he bashed Groff on the temple and shoved Belcher at the counter. Both men prepared to close in again but were riveted in place by a commanding voice from the doorway.

"Cease and desist! What is the meaning of this outrage?"

Into the store hustled Major Canby, an adjutant, and a pair

of troopers. Canby had one hand on the hilt of his saber and another on the flap to his holster. "I tolerate no brawling on this post," he said, addressing the scouts. "Both of you know that."

Groff stabbed a finger at Fargo. "Don't blame us. He started it by hittin' me."

"Is this true?" the officer demanded.

Before Fargo could answer, Diane Marsten stepped to the middle of the room. "Major, who threw the first punch is irrelevant. It was Mr. Groff and his friend who marched in here and caused a commotion. They have been giving me a hard time ever since I told Mr. Groff we do not want his services."

Major Canby frowned. "I was there. Mr. Groff, she made that abundantly clear. Why can't you take no for an answer?"

Groff did not respond. Belcher looked as if he had something to say but a sharp look from Groff stilled his tongue.

"Consider yourself on report," Major Canby said. "Since you are a civilian, the punishment I can inflict is limited. But I can and will dock you a month's pay if there is one more incident like this. Understood?"

"Yes, sir," Groff said sullenly. "Trust me. It won't happen again." Brusquely shouldering past Fargo, he marched from the building, his partner in tow.

Canby picked up Fargo's hat, which had fallen off during the fight, and gave it back. "Sometimes I swear that man is more trouble than he's worth. If he wasn't one of the best trackers in these parts, I'd kick him off the post and be done with him." Canby sighed. "When he heard that the ladies were willing to pay top dollar for their guide, he volunteered to lead them himself. He just can't take no for an answer, I suppose."

"No harm was done," Fargo said, rubbing a bump on his jaw.

Diane Marsten came over and lightly brushed her finger over the same spot. "You'll have a few nasty bruises by tomorrow," she said. "But you handled yourself quite well. I'll feel perfectly safe in your hands once we're on the trail." Her rosy lips curled in an enigmatic smile and she sashayed outside.

Major Canby shook his head. "Damned if I know what to make of that one. She dresses like a man and bosses men around as if she's God's gift to Creation, yet she's all woman under the skin."

Fargo had reached the same conclusion.

"That other one, though," Canby went on. "She's a nervous biddy, if you ask me. As high-strung as a mustang. Any man who lays a hand on her is liable to have his eyes scratched out."

"Maybe," Fargo allowed. But he had a hunch there was a lot more to Hester Williams than met the eye, and what met the eye was enough to make any man hunger for a taste of her lavish charms.

"Well, I'll leave you be for now. If you want, you're welcome to bunk in the barracks with the enlisted men. I'm sure none of them will mind."

Fargo recalled the last time he had slept in an army bed. The mattress—if you could call it that—had been as lumpy as a sack of coal and as hard as a log. The pillow had given off unpleasant odors. And the blankets had been paper thin. "I'm obliged," he said, "but I'd rather sleep out under the stars."

"Try the stable, then, or maybe out back by the woodshed," the major suggested, and turned to go. "Oh. I almost forgot. I wanted to warn you about a problem we've been having. Indian trouble. There's an Ute by the name of—"

"Red Band?" Fargo guessed.

"Yes. How did you know?"

Fargo detailed his encounter, concluding with, "I've been meaning to ask you about him. Why is he so interested in white women?"

Canby was disturbed by the news. "Damn him!" he exploded. "I warned him what would happen if he persisted on his mad search, but he won't listen. I'm afraid I'll have to send out patrols to bring him in, which might antagonize the whole tribe. It could result in open warfare."

The sutler, who had been listening to the conversation, snorted and said, "You should have brought him in after that incident with Malcolm. I know that buck. He won't rest until he gets his hands on a white gal." The sutler glanced at Fargo. "If I were you, friend, I'd make those ladies change their minds about the survey. It ain't safe."

Major Canby moved to the counter and leaned against it. He had the air of a man under a lot of strain. "I tried that myself, but they refused to listen. And my orders are explicit. In no way am I to hinder them in their efforts."

"You still haven't told me what's going on," Fargo prompted.

The officer's expression grew pained at the events he related. "About a month ago Red Band showed up at the fort. He had his wife along and she was deathly sick. High fever, chills, unable to keep food down, and as pale as a ghost. It seems his own people had done all they could for her and nothing helped. None of their herbs had an effect. So, as a last resort, Red Band brought Morning Dove here."

"He must have been desperate," the sutler interjected. "Red Band never has been very fond of our kind."

Canby continued. "I had our post physician do all he could, which wasn't much, I'm sad to say. She was too far gone. Two days after Red Band brought her in, Morning Dove died."

Again the sutler embellished the account. "And that whole time, Red Band sat in front of the infirmary like a statue. Never moved. Never talked. Hardly ever blinked. Damnedest thing I ever saw."

"I tried to explain to him there was nothing we could do," Major Canby said. "But he took it hard, real hard. Somehow he'd gotten the notion into his head that white men could cure just about anything, that our medicine was all-powerful. So he blamed us for her death. Claimed we hadn't done all we could, that we wanted her to die." Canby smacked his right fist against his left palm. "Sheer nonsense. But try to talk reason to a man who has just lost the woman he loved."

"And now he wants a white woman?" Fargo quizzed them.

The sutler swore. "He's taken a page from Scripture, the heathen. An eye for an eye, a tooth for a tooth. Only in this case, Red Band wants a white gal to make up for the wife he thinks we took from him."

"Utterly ridiculous," Major Canby said, "but there you have it. Two weeks ago he showed up at a settler's. Malcolm is the man's name. Red Band tried to steal Malcolm's wife but Malcolm and his three sons drove the Utes off with rifle fire." He worriedly rubbed his chin. "Now this business with you. To be honest, I'm worried where it will lead. A war with the Utes must be averted at all costs." Looking up, he remarked, "It would take a tremendous load off my shoulders if you could convince the professors to postpone their trek."

"I'll try," Fargo said. He got his chance a few minutes later, after he emerged from the store and spotted Diane Marsten over by the wagons. She bestowed a cooly reserved smile as he approached, a smile that evaporated with the first words out of his mouth.

"I've been talking to the major—"

"Let me guess," she said. "It's about that Indian, isn't it? I'll tell you the same thing I told Canby. We're under a time constraint. In order to complete our survey on schedule, we must start right away. I seriously doubt the stupid Ute is within a hundred miles of Fort Bridger."

"I ran into him a short ways south of here—" Fargo began, but she did not let him finish.

"Ah. *South* of the post. Ute country, I understand, is to the south. So is Ira Malcolm's homestead. Since we're traveling to the north, we have nothing to fear. That is, unless you happen to be afraid."

Fargo did not let her get his goat. "Fear has nothing to do with it. No one in their right mind sticks their head into the steel jaws of an open bear trap."

"Are you saying you've changed your mind? You're not man enough to guide us now?" Diane's eyes filled with contempt, and something else.

Right then and there would have been the sensible time to pull out. Fargo was perfectly justified in refusing to go. But he had told them he would, and he was a man of his word. "I'll guide you, lady. Just don't blame me if you or your friend wind up spending the rest of your days in a Ute lodge."

"We can take care of ourselves," Diane boasted. "As for

Hester, I think you have the wrong impression. We're acquaintances, not close friends. Professional rivals would be a better term. For an Albany graduate, she's fairly competent."

"I don't follow you."

"Hester went to Albany, I went to Oberlin." Diane said it as if going to Oberlin were somehow special, as if it made her better than Hester Williams. "As everyone knows, Oberlin is the best institution of higher learning on the planet. No matter what those conceited Harvard grads claim."

Marsten walked off, leaving Fargo to ponder exactly what he had gotten himself into. Taking two temperamental fillies into the dark heart of the savage wilderness, with a roving band of hostile Utes on the loose, was a surefire invitation for trouble. Shaking his head, he went to break the bad news to Canby.

The major had left the store. Fargo ambled toward the headquarters building, passing others along the way. He had just gone by the guardhouse and was abreast of a narrow gap between it and the quartermaster's when a slight sound made him glance into the shadows. He registered a dim shape a split second before he saw a knife flash out of the gap toward his chest.

Most anyone else would have been caught flat-footed. The glittering blade streaked into the sunlight like a bolt of steel lightning. Fargo twisted in that self-same instant, and the knife missed him by the width of the whang it nicked. In twisting he lost his balance and fell. His right hand dropped to his Colt, sweeping it out. He cocked the hammer and swiveled toward the gap, only to find the shadowy shape gone.

Rising, Fargo ran between the buildings. He slowed near the other end, listening for telltale footfalls, but there were none. Peeking out, he saw a knot of soldiers sixty feet away. Several others were engaged in various tasks, but none were near enough to have been responsible for the attempt on his life. He stepped into the open and looked both ways. In a corral at the rear of the stable some horses milled. Behind the mess hall a private peeled potatoes.

Fargo had a good idea who had thrown the knife but no idea

where Groff had gone. Twirling the Colt into his holster, he retraced his steps. The weapon lay in the dirt. It was a butcher, as the frontiersmen called them, a favorite for skinning and scalping and such. The long blade was razor sharp. The original handle had been removed and replaced by smooth bone grips. While not a true throwing knife, it had excellent balance and heft.

Wedging it under his belt, Fargo prowled the post seeking Groff and Belcher. Neither was to be found. It wasn't until sunset that he learned Major Canby had sent them out with a patrol to hunt down Red Band and bring him back to Fort Bridger.

The officer invited Fargo to eat at the mess hall. They were joined by the two professors, Upton Clark, and the fourth expedition member, a scruffy man in ill-fitting store-bought clothes who was introduced as Bitterroot John. They sat at a broad table at the head of the cramped room.

Every trooper who filed by was mesmerized by the two women, as well they should be. The fairer sex were as scarce as hen's teeth on the frontier. For every female, there were a thousand lonely males pining for womanly companionship.

Fargo saw the envy in the eyes of the soldiers, and had to smile. If the boys in blue only knew. For the better part of an hour he had suffered through a long-winded talk by Marsten and Williams about how indispensable a theodolite was to a surveyor. They rambled on and on about how to use the device to measure horizontal and vertical angles. Major Canby and Upton Clark were either extremely polite or really interested, but he was bored as could be. His smile did not go unnoticed.

"Do you find our discussion amusing, Mr. Fargo?" Hester Williams asked.

"I was just thinking that if Red Band shows up, you can beat him over the head with your theodolites," Fargo said, and took a bite of a cracker. A stale, salty cracker, typical fare by military standards. Army food was so poor, it was a standing joke among the enlisted men that more of them were killed by their own cooks than by Indians. But it wasn't fair to blame the men who had to fix the food. They had little to work with. Rations consisted of hardtack, beans, bacon, coarse bread, and low-grade beef when it was available. Bacon often arrived already rancid, flour might be infested with mice or insects, and the hardtack was sometimes so hard that a man could not make a dent in it if he gnawed on the stuff for a month.

"How droll," Hester responded. "But we're counting on you to safeguard us if we're attacked."

"There are fourteen warriors in Red Band's bunch, counting him," Fargo mentioned. "I'm just one man. There's only so much I can do."

Diane Marsten stirred. "Hester and I will defend ourselves, if need be. And Clark has shot grouse and ducks." She shifted toward Bitterroot John. "What about you, Mr. Weatherbee? Have you any experience fighting Indians?"

All during the meal Bitterroot John had been cramming food into his mouth as if his stomach were a bottomless pit. Now he froze with his mouth stuffed with crackers, then tried to swallow and nearly gagged. "Sorry," he said, wiping broken bits from his mouth with the back of his hand. "Generally speakin', ma'am, I have more experience runnin' from Injuns than I do fightin' 'em."

"You admit to being a coward?" Diane said curtly.

"Well, now, I wouldn't be so quick to judge, were I you." Bitterroot John picked up his glass and gulped greedily. Some of the water spilled over his lower lip and down his chin. "Fact is, ma'am," he said, "stayin' shy of those red devils is just plain smart. I've done me some trappin' and buffalo huntin', and I've seen more than a few pards of mine after the Injuns got done with 'em. Trust me. It ain't a pretty sight."

"But you will fight if you have to?" Hester pressed him.

"If I had my druthers, no," Bitterroot John said. "If I'm trapped with no other choice, then I'd have to, wouldn't I?" He shrugged. "Shucks, ladies. I know my limitations. I ain't no soldier. And I ain't like Mr. Fargo, here. They say he licks grizzlies with his bare hands and can drop an Injun with one shot from a mile off."

Diane Marsten's hooded eyes fixed on Fargo. "Yes, I've

heard those tall tales. Along with others that were much more interesting."

What was she hinting at? the Trailsman wondered. He'd heard the same stories himself. Stories about fights he had never been in, about exploits he'd never had. Thankfully, they weren't as wild and woolly as those told about other frontiersmen. Like Davy Crockett, for instance. Yearly almanacs pretended to tout Crockett's real-life adventures, stories so silly Fargo could not understand why anyone bothered to read them. Who would ever believe that a man could wade the Mississippi or leap the Ohio? One almanac claimed the famed Tennessean could ride streaks of lightning and wring the tails off of comets.

Major Canby cleared his throat. "Professor Marsten, you've put me in a bind. I can't stop you from leaving, although I wish heart and soul you wouldn't go. So to insure you are not molested, I plan to send a dozen troopers under the command of Lieutenant Jacobson north with you tomorrow."

"I thank you, but it's not necessary," Diane said.

"Please. For my own peace of mind," Canby insisted. "Allow me to send the escort."

Clark Upton finally had something to say. "If our party is too large, we'll scare off every animal within miles. The smaller, the better for me, Major. I intend to study the local wildlife, remember?"

"It's only a dozen men," the officer stressed.

Hester Williams gave a wave of her hand. "A few days will be all right, I suppose. But after that, if no Utes have appeared, I recommend the lieutenant return to the post and let us get on with our work unhindered."

Fargo was not asked his opinion and did not offer it. He had already warned Diane Marsten of the possible consequences. For college-educated women, the two professors were more pigheaded than a politician. Maybe the college education had something to do with it. He'd met people like them before. People who thought they were so damn smart, they knew all there was to know. No one could talk any sense into them.

Presently the meal ended. The ladies excused themselves.

Fargo strolled out into the cool evening air and hooked his thumbs in his gunbelt. Stars twinkled overhead. The post was quiet, or as quiet as it got. Most of the enlisted men were relaxing in the barracks after a grueling day. Sentries patrolled the walls. Two were on guard at the gate, which was always closed after dark.

Fargo collected his bedroll and his rifle and made for the rear of the compound. Beside a large shack in which chopped wood was stored during the winter he found a low overhang. He spread out his blankets underneath, set his saddlebags nearby, and prepared to turn in early. About to lie down, he was mildly surprised to see Clark Upton hastening over.

"Good evening, Mr. Fargo. A word with you, if I may?" Not waiting for an answer, the naturalist asked, "Did you perhaps pick up my watch by mistake during supper?"

Fargo propped himself on an elbow. First Diane Marsten hinted he was yellow, now this. "Take some advice. Out here a man can be shot if he goes around accusing others of being a thief."

Upton glanced around to verify they were alone. "I'm not blaming you, sir. I merely wanted to be certain. You see, I have my suspicions. In the past few days I've lost two pens, a pocketknife, and now my watch." Upton bent down. "Just between you and me, I suspect our cook. Please keep an eye on Bitterroot John on the trail. I don't trust him as far as I can throw him."

Upton bustled off, mumbling to himself, leaving Fargo to mull the wisdom of venturing into the wilderness with two contrary females, a petty thief, and a boneheaded animal lover who was more interested in studying wild creatures than in the safety of his own hide. "If I had any brains I'd back out while I still can," he said aloud.

The next moment, as Fargo went to lie down, an iron forearm looped around his throat and clamped it as tight as a vise.

# 4

It happened so swiftly that Skye Fargo's windpipe was choked off before he could suck a breath into his lungs. Heaving up off the ground, he tried to break free but the man who had the choke grip was immensely strong. Fargo twisted to the right and left. He drove his elbows back. He kicked at the other man's shins. Nothing worked. The pressure on his throat grew greater and greater, the pain worse and worse.

"Got you now, bastard!"

The voice was Groff's! Fargo grasped the scout's forearm, tucked at the waist, and snapped forward, flipping Groff clear over his back and breaking the hold at last. Gasping for air, Fargo backpedaled to give himself room to maneuver. The scout surged after him. A tomahawk cleaved the air, sizzling past Fargo's ear.

"I'm fixin' to kill you, Trailsman, and have it blamed on the Utes," Groff boasted.

Fargo evaded a savage swing, then another. Slowly but steadily Groff forced him back toward the palisade. When his back bumped into it, the scout grinned wickedly and sheared the tomahawk at his head. Fargo ducked, heard the weapon *thunk* into the wood, then lashed out, slamming his fist into Groff's jaw. The scout staggered, growled, and attacked again, swinging wildly.

"Die, damn you!"

Fargo skipped to the left, barely avoiding a blow that would have sheared his arm off at the shoulder. Groff was incensed, fighting recklessly, which made him all the more dangerous. Bounding out of reach, Fargo palmed the Colt, but as he drew,

Groff lunged. The tomahawk smashed against the pistol, jarring it from Fargo's fingers.

"No you don't!" the scout hissed.

Fargo pivoted, sidestepped, leaped, always staying one step ahead. They were now under the overhang, near the shed. Propped against it was a rake. Feinting to the left, Fargo went right. He grasped the long handle and spun, elevating the rake just as the tomahawk arced down at the crown of his skull. The tomahawk was deflected. Shifting, Fargo drove the end of the handle into Groff's gut and had the satisfaction of hearing Groff grunt and gurgle.

"Son of a bitch!" the scout snarled. Crouching, he came in low and fast, raining blow after blow, a human whirlwind intent on chopping Fargo into bits and pieces.

No soldiers were in the vicinity. None of the sentries were nearby. Fargo was on his own. Groff had picked the ideal moment to strike, and unless Fargo came up with a brainstorm soon, the tomahawk would burst him open like an overripe melon.

Again and again Groff swung. Again and again Fargo countered with the rake handle. In the flurry of hectic movement they wound up in front of the shed door. It was partially open. Which gave Fargo an idea. He dodged a slice to the chest, rammed the rake against Groff's shoulder, and while Groff was briefly off balance, he plunged into the shed and shoved the door shut.

Now the only way for Groff to get at him was to come through the door. Fargo put his shoulder to it, waiting for loud thuds to ensue. Let Groff hack at the door all he wanted. The noise was bound to bring guards on the run.

But nothing happened. The tomahawk did not embed itself. Groff did not utter a sound. Wary of a ruse, Fargo pressed an ear to the panel. Total silence reigned outside. Since there were no windows, the only way to find out what was going on was for Fargo to crack the door and peek out. The area in front of the shed was deserted. Apparently, Groff had gone.

Fargo was still suspicious. The scout was not the type to give up so easily. He peered toward the corners of the shed, then scanned the space under the overhang. No Groff. Holding the rake in front of him, Fargo eased the door wide enough to step out. No one hurtled at him from out of the gloom. It was as if the earth had yawned wide and swallowed the scout whole.

Fargo took several slow steps. When it did not spark a response, he lowered the rake and scratched his head. *Where could Groff have gotten to?* he wondered. The scrape of a boot heel on wood gave him a clue. Fargo whirled. Somehow Groff had clambered on top of the overhang. The scout was in midair, the tomahawk hoisted to split Fargo's head.

Fargo threw himself to the left but he was a fraction too slow. The tomahawk flashed down. By sheer accident it connected with the rake handle, not with him, splitting the handle in half and sparing him serious injury. Skipping to the rear, he looked around for something else to use.

"You have more lives than a stinkin' cat," Groff fumed.

Then Fargo spied his Colt lying a couple of yards away. It was closer to him than it was to the scout. Taking a gamble, he flung himself at it, diving and snatching the revolver up in a smooth forward roll that brought him into a crouch with it cocked and extended. Only, there was no one to shoot.

Groff was disappearing around the far corner of the woodshed. Venting an oath, Fargo gave chase. As he cleared the corner he saw the scout scuttling up a ladder to the parapet. Fargo banged off a shot from the hip but knew he missed. Shouts broke out as he reached the ladder and climbed. For an instant he glimpsed Groff poised at the top of the stockade wall, about to go over the side. The scout fixed a baleful glare and hollered, "We'll meet again!" and dropped from view.

Someone was bellowing for the corporal of the guard as Fargo gained the parapet and rushed to the spot where Groff had gone over. Twenty yards out a pair of horsemen were riding like the wind, horsemen in buckskins. Taunting laughter mocked Fargo. He raised the Colt but the two scouts vanished into the night.

"Damn."

Sentries came on the run. So did a dozen other enlisted men,

noncoms, and officers, from all corners of the post. They besieged Fargo with questions, jabbering all at once. He ignored
them. As he was replacing the spent cartridge, Major Canby
materialized at the bottom of the ladder and craned his neck
upward. "What's going on? Who fired that shot?"

Fargo descended. "I thought you told me Groff was out with
a patrol?"

"He is. Belcher and him, both. Why?"

"He just tried to kill me."

"Impossible. Both scouts are under orders to stay with Captain Gleason's unit until they have apprehended Red Band or
run low on rations. You must be mistaken."

"Not unless Groff has a twin brother, I'm not," Fargo
walked toward the shed, pondering. It would not have been
hard for Groff and Belcher to slip away from the patrol on
some pretext or another and circle back around to the post.
Since they knew the guards' routine, sneaking unseen into the
fort would be child's play.

Major Canby dogged his heels. "Could you have been mistaken? Could it have been someone else you mistook for
Groff? An Indian, maybe?"

Fargo halted so abruptly that Canby nearly collided with
him. "When someone is trying to bury a tomahawk in your
noggin, you tend to notice little things like who it is."

"All right. I can't let this pass like I did the incident at the
sutler's. Attempted murder is a grave offense. I'll have Groff
apprehended and convene a formal hearing. It will be your
word against his, but if he can't account for himself, I'll recommend a trial be held."

"You'll do no such thing."

"What? Why not?"

Fargo was back at the overhang. Hunkering, he began to
smooth his rumpled blankets. "I don't want Groff behind bars.
I want him free so he can try again."

"Are you insane? He's not the sort you should trifle with.
They say he's killed four or five men and more Indians than
you can shake a stick at. Don't take him lightly." Canby
waited for Fargo to respond, and when he didn't, the major

became irritated. "Damn it, man. What do you have in mind? Why set yourself up as bait?"

"So he'll take the hook."

"You want him to kill you?"

"I want him to *try*." Fargo glanced up.

"Oh," Major Canby said, comprehension dawning. "Oh," he repeated, sounding worried. "But think of the risk you're taking."

"Major, if you put him behind bars, he'll get out again someday. And probably come looking for me. I'd rather settle it sooner than later. Once and for all."

"Yes, I see." Canby coughed, fidgeted, then said. "But if I let you do as you want, I'm condoning the very thing I want to prosecute Groff for."

"Are you? If you were out in the mountains and a rabid wolf jumped you, would you defend yourself?"

"Yes, yes. I see your point. Still—" Canby stopped and gazed wistfully at the sky. "I'm from Vermont, Mr. Fargo. From a very small town in the country. I've been a soldier for over ten years and I've seen more than my share of atrocities, but there are some things a man never grows accustomed to. Do you understand?"

"Yes."

Canby seemed not to hear. "All the senseless bloodshed. Indians butchering whites. Whites butchering Indians. Whites slaying other whites in cold blood. It gets to a man. Eats at his soul. I'm a warrior by choice, and warriors spill blood, but I like to think I do so with honor."

The major departed. Fargo was about to lie down when a vague shape detached itself from the deep shadow at the base of the palisade. In a twinkling the Colt was in his hand. "Step out where I can see you," he commanded.

"Don't shoot, Skye. I'm quite friendly." In the starlight Diane Marsten was exquisitely lovely. Her golden hair framed her finely chiseled features like a halo. A thick robe was wrapped tight around her lush body, accenting the peaks and valleys in all the right places. "I couldn't help but hear the commotion."

Fargo replaced the six-gun. Above them a sentry paced back and forth, no doubt under orders to insure no more attempts were made on his life. "I figured you would be asleep by now. We have a long day ahead of us."

Diane came to the edge of the blanket. The breeze bore with it the fragrant scent of her perfume. Her lips were sparkling rubies, her eyes gleaming sapphires. Her breasts jutted against the folds of the robe, alluring, inviting. "Care if we talk awhile?"

Fargo gestured. She carefully lowered herself, tucking her long legs. Well out of his reach, he observed wryly. "What about?"

"You perhaps." Diane paused much too long. "Do you have a wife hidden somewhere, by chance? Or a squaw stashed away in some wretched village?"

"Indian women don't like to be called squaws," Fargo mentioned. "It makes them seem less than they are."

"And what are they, exactly?"

"People, like you and me. There are good ones and bad ones, just as there are good whites and whites who aren't worth a damn."

"Are you referring to our mutual acquaintance, Mr. Groff?"

"He's snake-mean, but he's not half as tough as he thinks he is. Compared to some of the hardcases I've met, Groff is downright tame." Fargo reclined on his left side so he could resort to the Colt if need be.

"Intriguing," Diane said. "There is more depth to your character than I was led to believe. Rumor has it that your only interests are women, whiskey, and cards."

"The rumor is true," Fargo said, and thought of a saying appropriate for someone who prided herself on her college education. "Never judge a book by its cover."

"Touché." She grinned and rested a hand on the blanket. "You're not half as shallow as I thought you would be. Our trip to the Wind River Range promises to be quite interesting." Her hand drifted across her robe and it mysteriously came partly undone, revealing a generous expanse of her beautiful globes.

Fargo felt his mouth water. A keen hunger filled him, a craving that had nothing to do with food. He started to lean toward her but was brought up short by the heavy clomp-clomp-clomp of the sentry's boots. It was hardly the right time or place. Much to his regret. "What about you? Have a beau back East waiting to take you for his bride?"

Diane laughed merrily. "Me? Marry? What a quaint notion. But I seriously doubt I'll ever find a suitable prospect. The qualities I want in a man are in short supply."

"What might they be?"

She ticked them off on her fingers. "I want someone who is highly intelligent. A person with an outstanding sense of humor. A man who is a witty conversationalist. Looks aren't all that important, but I prefer he be tall, muscular, and virile. Someone who is aggressive. Someone with a shrewd business sense. Oh. And someone with lots and lots of money."

"Is that all?"

Marsten actually reflected a bit. "I'd like him to be considerate of others. Compassionate to the needy. Someone with a few degrees under his belt would be nice, just so we can relate as equals." She pursed those ruby lips. "Yes, I think that's about it."

"You don't ask much, lady."

"Why? What's wrong with wanting special traits in a mate? It's no different from looking for certain qualities in a horse you'd want to buy."

"Horses aren't humans. You're mixing apples and oranges."

Diane's mouth pinched together. "Why? Because I demand the same perfection in men that men have always demanded in me?"

"How's that?"

"If you were female, you wouldn't need to ask." She gazed across the post. "You have no idea what it is like to be a woman in a man's world. Women have to try harder at everything. We're held to a higher standard. So if we want to compete with men on their own terms, we have to be twice as competent as they are."

"Back in the East it might be true. Not west of the Mississippi."

"You don't honestly believe that."

Fargo rested on his elbows. "Out here a woman is measured by how well she holds her own. She doesn't need to be better than a man. She just has to do the things expected of her and do them well." The skepticism that etched Diane's face prompted him to go on. "A settler doesn't care how many degrees his wife has. He doesn't care if she can speak Latin or quote poetry. All he cares about is whether she can cook and sew and mend the kids when they're sick."

"Cooking and sewing," Marsten said sarcastically. "Drudgery, plain and simple."

"And what do you call spending ten hours a day behind a plow? Or chopping wood until your shoulders ache so bad you can't move your arms? In the West life is hard on men *and* women. All they ask of each other is that they hold up their end of the work."

For over a minute Diane sat in quiet thought. "Still waters do run deep," she commented at length. Impulsively, she reached out and brushed her hand over his. Then, jerking her arm back, she rose and hurried into the darkness.

Fargo stretched out, propped his head in his hands, and grinned. She had been right about one thing, at least. Their journey promised to be much more interesting than he had reckoned on. He closed his eyes, doubtful he would fall asleep for a while, not with his nerves still on edge over what had happened. Hardly had the thought passed through his mind than slumber claimed him. He dreamed of Groff, a giant, hulking Groff who tried to stomp him into the dirt as if he were a bug.

The clink of metal against wood woke Fargo with a start. He sat up, fully alert, producing the Colt. He was all alone. No one else was abroad. His internal clock told him dawn was not far off. Rising, he relieved the kinks in his arms and legs, then moved out from under the overhang.

Up on the rampart the sentry was fiddling with his rifle. He waved, so Fargo returned the favor. Gathering his effects, he moseyed toward the corral. Well before a pink tinge splashed the eastern horizon with color, he had the Ovaro saddled and ready to go. He had counted on leaving at first light but it was not to be. Clark Upton was up early enough but then had to shave and wash and eat a hearty breakfast. The two women were worse. Neither stepped from the quarters Canby had graciously given them until the sun was half an hour high into the sky.

Only Bitterroot John was set to leave at the crack of dawn. Without being asked, he hooked up the teams and moved the wagons close to the gate.

Major Canby came out to see them off. The junior officer he had picked to head their escort, Lieutenant Jacobson, was a gangly spit-and-polish soldier who became tongue-tied around the female professors. The dozen troopers were more bored than anything else. To them, safeguarding the survey crew was just part of their regular duty. And they were not particularly anxious to leave the relative safety and comfort of the fort.

Fargo and Jacobson took the lead. Upton Clark rode with Bitterroot John in the first wagon. Diane and Hester handled the second, Diane working the reins. With the troopers bringing up the rear, they filed from Fort Bridger.

Fargo had the route worked out in his head. He guided them north along the Green River, always paralleling it so they would not want for water. The broad basin through which the river wound was carpeted by a sea of short grass dotted here and there by islands of trees. Belts of sage broke the monotony. Wildlife was plentiful, but the animals tended to keep their distance. Antelope went bounding off in tremendous leaps that dazzled the eye. Deer would stare, then take flight with tails erect. Jackrabbits were so abundant that Fargo planned on having rabbit stew for supper unless he had a shot at larger game.

The morning was uneventful. Lieutenant Jacobson was a laconic man who seldom spoke unless spoken to, which suited Fargo just fine. When the sun was directly overhead Fargo called a brief halt to water and rest the horses. The spot he picked was thick with cottonwoods, which afforded comforting shade. He sat with his back propped against a smooth bole and munched on a piece of pemmican.

Clark Upton was over by a patch of flowers besieged by butterflies. Pencil and paper in hand, he was sketching, whistling to himself while he worked, as happy as the proverbial lark. Bitterroot John was treating himself to a chaw of tobacco. The troopers were lounging, grateful for the break. Lieutenant Jacobson had joined them and was examining a private's mount.

Fargo leaned back, closed his eyes, and let the sun warm his face and chest. Upton and the professors might not like having the soldiers for nursemaids, but he was glad Canby had insisted the detail tag along. The major knew what he was doing.

Indians weren't fools, no matter what most whites believed. Nor were they as ruthlessly bloodthirsty as they were painted. They rarely attacked if they thought it would cost a lot of lives. The presence of the troopers would make Red Band or any other hostile think twice about causing trouble.

Footsteps drew near. Fargo did not need to open his eyes to tell who it was. Perfume was enough of a clue. "What can I do for you, ladies?"

"How did—?" Diane Marsten said, and caught herself. "We wanted to let you know that in a couple of hours we must stop and set up a theodolite."

"We have to get our bearings, as it were," Hester Williams elaborated, "so our logs will be accurate from here on out. One slip, one little mistake, and it can throw off the whole project. The government is counting on us to get this job done right."

"Whatever you want," Fargo said. "But there are three rules I expect you to follow at all times."

"Rules?" Hester said.

"Never leave camp without telling someone where you are going. Never go alone. And always take a pistol and a rifle."

"Must we? I've already told you I don't like firearms," Hester reminded him. "The world would be much better off without them. Were it up to me, I'd gather every last gun and melt them all down into plowshares."

"What would that prove?"

"Why, what a silly question. Without guns, people wouldn't kill each other anymore. Whites and Indians would have to get along whether they wanted to or not."

Fargo opened his eyes and read her expression. Damned if she wasn't serious. "One of us is silly, that's for sure," he commented. How was it, he asked himself, that people who spent years in hard study to sharpen their minds ended up so dull-witted?

Hester tilted her cute nose upward. "I'd expect no less from a ruffian who struts around with a revolver strapped to his hip. Do you like the feeling of power it gives you? Do you like being able to decide who will live and who will die simply by squeezing the trigger?"

"No, lady. I like breathing."

"You're being facetious."

Fargo patted his Colt. "This is a tool, Professor Williams. Like my knife and my rope and my rifle. A tool that helps me go on breathing, day in and day out. I don't like to kill, but when someone or something is trying to make wolf meat of me, then this pistol comes in mighty handy."

"Exactly my point. If there were no firearms, imagine how much less killing there would be in the world."

"Did a horse stomp on your head when you were in diapers?" Fargo quipped. There was only so much stupidity a man could take. "People were slaughtering each another long before guns were invented. Take away every last pistol and rifle and they'll go back to using knives, swords, and clubs."

Diane Marsten smiled. "I think what Mr. Fargo is trying to say, Hester, is that humans are predators at heart. Our natures are more akin to the wolf and the cougar than to the lamb. We kill because an innate drive deep inside of us compels us to, because survival at all costs is ingrained into the fabric of who and what we are. Isn't that true, Skye?"

Fargo shook his head in amazement. It was peculiar how a pair of learned academics could take simple things and make them so complicated. "Just do as I told you. If you want to go on living, take a gun when you go on a survey."

"If you insist," Hester said irritably. She marched off with her chin in the air. For a grown woman, she acted more like the last ten-year-old Fargo had met.

Diane Marsten was amused. "Keep charming her like you do. I think that secretly Hester is quite fond of you." She chortled. "It isn't often a man will talk back to her. Most are too intimidated by her looks or her brains, or both."

"The same hold true with you?"

The blonde hunkered and plucked a blade of grass before answering. "Yes, I'm sorry to admit. Men are afraid of strong women. They see us as a threat, so they want nothing to do with us."

"There you go again. Branding all men with a brand fit only for a few." Fargo swallowed the last of the pemmican. "Did you ever think that being strong might have nothing to do with it."

"What else could be to blame?" Diane asked, legitimately interested. "I know it's not my imagination. I've seen the same attitude time and time again. So why else would men give me the cold shoulder?"

"No man likes to have a woman lead him around on a leash."

Professor Marsten stiffened. "Be blunt. Are you saying I'm a bit of a bitch?"

"More than a bit."

Drawing back her hand, Diane aimed a slap at his cheek but Fargo caught her wrist and held fast. "You—! You—!" she sputtered, at a loss for words that would do her fury justice. They locked eyes.

"You asked me, remember? If I'm not telling the truth, then you can hit me," Fargo said. "But if I'm not telling you something you haven't heard before, maybe you should take a good look at yourself." Relaxing his grip, he sat back to await her reply.

At that moment a high-pitched shriek shattered the tranquil scene. Hester Williams was on one knee at the water's edge, frozen in the act of splashing her arms and neck to cool off. On the opposite bank, towering on two legs, was the one creature no frontiersman ever wanted to tangle with, a beast rightly ranked as the most formidable alive.

"Oh my God!" Diane declared. "A grizzly!"

# 5

Skye Fargo was on his feet and moving swiftly toward Hester Williams before her cry faded. Another such scream might provoke the bear into crossing over. So far it was merely curious, its nose flaring as it tested the breeze. Over eight feet tall and as massive as a bull, it was a young male not quite in its prime. "Don't move," he whispered to Hester. "Don't yell."

"It's so big!" she marveled.

"I've seen bigger." Fargo talked softly to soothe her and to avoid arousing the bear. Thankfully, none of the troopers were anxious to test the grizzly's mettle. They stood in an awed knot, awaiting orders from their equally flabbergasted officer. Bitterroot John was on the seat of the first wagon, picking at his teeth with a twig and acting as unconcerned as if he were seated on a bench back at the fort.

"I didn't know," Hester said as Fargo reached her and draped an arm over her shoulder. "Why, that thing could crush my skull with a single swipe of its paw."

"Or one bite of those jaws," Fargo mentioned. "Just stay still. If it's not hungry and if it doesn't see us as a threat, it will move on." He wished that he had the Henry but it was in the scabbard on his saddle.

The bear sniffed loudly, then started to lower onto all fours and turn away. Suddenly a jubilant bellow brought it up onto its hind legs again.

"My word! What a magnificent specimen! Who cares about drawing butterflies when a bear like that has paid us a visit!" Clark Upton dashed to the edge of the river, his pencil and pad pressed to his chest in rapture. "Look at him! Isn't he grand?

I'll wade out as far as I can and sketch him before he wanders off."

"Stand still," Fargo warned, but he might as well have been talking to an adobe wall. The naturalist was so excited that he barreled into the Green River and strode on out, his pencil flying over a sheet of paper.

"I must capture every detail, every nuance," Upton was saying, more to himself than to anyone else. "This will make a remarkable addition to my collection. Fit for public display, I should think."

Moving to the river's edge, Fargo beckoned. "Come back here, you jackass, before it's too late."

Upton was oblivious to everything except the bear. "Look at how big he is! The breadth of those shoulders! The length of those claws! And such a healthy, lustrous coat! Beautiful. Simply beautiful."

One man's beauty was another man's nightmare. Fargo saw the grizzly lower itself and step into the Green River. Head high, it advanced toward Clark Upton, who mindlessly kept on walking and grinning as if the bear were a harmless puppy instead of a living engine of steel-sinewed destruction. Fargo waded in after the naturalist, the sluggish current not impeding him half as much as the soft muddy bottom. He had to go a couple of yards before firm gravel gave him solid footing. By then Upton was twenty feet away, drawing at a furious pace as the grizzly lumbered steadily forward. "Stop!" Fargo warned.

Upton waved a hand in dismissal of the notion and slowly pressed on, so intent on his artistry that he nearly went under when he stumbled into a sink hole. Spitting and flailing, he was able to regain his footing. "Thank goodness!" he said, running a palm over the page. "I almost got this wet."

In another minute that was going to be the least of the man's worries. Fargo hurried, but the bear was going faster now, plowing through the water with ease, its huge head lowered, its great hump rippling with raw power. "Clark! Listen to me!"

"I almost have it," Upton replied, sketching feverishly. At long last he halted, perilously close to the oncoming monster.

"Don't worry. I've drawn bruins before. He won't harm me if I don't antagonize him."

Was stupidity contagious? Fargo wondered as he broke into a shuffling run. The water was as high as his thighs, resisting every step. Behind him Lieutenant Jacobson called out.

"Mr. Upton! Mr. Fargo! Get out of the way! Give my men a clear shot!"

The officer had lined up the troopers in two rows, the foremost on their knees. They were armed with Model 1855 tape lock muskets, standard issue to troops on the frontier. Single-shot weapons, the muskets had enough sheer stopping power to drop a man in his tracks but not enough to drop big game.

Fargo angled to the right, then discovered Upton had not moved. "Damn it, Clark! Get out of there!" he fumed, with no result. The soldiers were yelling. So were the women. Yet the naturalist continued to draw, glancing repeatedly from the sheet to the bear and back again.

Fargo whipped out the Colt and took deliberate aim. It was doubtful the shot would do more than anger the grizzly, but he had to do *something*. Then, amazingly, Clark Upton began to shuffle sideways, but in so doing, he blundered between Fargo and the bear. "Keep going! Keep going!" Fargo begged.

Upton looked over his shoulder and smiled as if to say everything was all right, he was perfectly safe. But he could not have been more wrong. He turned and seemed to finally realize how close the bear was. Standing stock-still, he showed true courage by not flinching when the grizzly came to a stop an arm's length away. The great bear tilted its enormous head and sniffed, not sure what to make of Upton, apparently.

Fargo held his breath. There was a chance, just a chance, the naturalist would live to relate his exploit. Provided the bear decided he was harmless and drifted elsewhere. The shouts had died. Everyone was glued to the scene, afraid to make a noise for fear of setting off the grizzly. For long, nerve-racking moments the bear studied Upton, until, uttering a snort, it started to turn back toward the opposite shore.

Fargo let out the breath and heard someone to his rear exhale loudly in relief. The worst was over. All they had to do was stay quiet until the grizzly was gone. He figured the two professors were most likely to do something dumb, and he was slowly swiveling toward them to signal for them to be still, when, incredibly, Clark Upton rotated toward *him* and beamed.

"See? I told you there was nothing to worry about. Animals are my stock in trade, so to speak. No one knows their habits like I do."

The boast was the last the naturalist ever made. In a blur, moving with astounding quickness for a creature so immense, the grizzly spun, raised its right forepaw out of the water, and smashed it against Clark Upton's head. The titanic force behind the blow ripped Upton's head from his neck with the same ease that Fargo might rip a flower from its stem. In a spray of scarlet, the head arced into the air and splashed down inches from where Fargo stood. The face was locked in disbelieving shock. Then the head sank like a rock and tumbled on downriver. The headless body swayed but did not fall. Not right away. Not until the grizzly batted it aside and stalked toward the Trailsman.

"Mr. Fargo! For God's sake! We can't shoot with you in the way!"

Fargo did not need to be reminded twice. He ran to the right, or tried to. Instantly, the bear came after him, but it was in no great rush. The great head bobbing, it closed at a leisurely pace. Lieutenant Jacobson's command to open fire cracked crisp and clear. So did the initial volley, twelve rifles blasting in unison. Fargo heard slugs smack home, saw the hide erupt in red geysers.

Venting a savage roar, the grizzly wheeled toward the troopers. They were reloading just as fast as they could. The bear charged, cleaving the water like a ship. Its maw was stretched agape to rend and slash, exposing its tapered teeth. Teeth capable of grinding solid bone into splinters.

Jacobson had his saber out. "Volley fire!" he bawled. "Front rank, on my order, fire!" The rifles thundered, the shots barely slowing the monster down. "Front rank, reload! Rear rank, at my command, fire!" Again a hail of lead tore into the bear.

Again it slowed down, but only momentarily. Roaring hideously, it narrowed the gap.

Two more volleys were fired before the grizzly reached the bank. The first caused it to totter, the second to keel forward, its front legs buckling. Growling and snapping at empty air, it sought to rise and reach its foes. Slugs had riddled it with so many holes its hide resembled a sieve gushing red rivulets. The bear floundered, righted itself, then sagged, half in and half out of the water, still alive but too weak to do more than gnash its huge jaws.

Fargo holstered his Colt in order to grab at Upton's body as the current caught hold. Snagging an arm, he hauled it toward the bank. The going was slow. The grisly headless remains seemed to weigh as much as the grizzly.

"Johnson! Kendall! Sirak!" Lieutenant Jacobson barked. "Jump in and give him a hand. Snap to!"

The three soldiers handed their rifles to companions and plunged in. Each gave the twitching silver tip a wide berth. With their help, Fargo soon had the body sprawled on a flat stretch of shoreline. Jagged strips of flesh hung from the ravaged neck. To look at it made even Fargo queasy, and he had seen more than his share of gore and butchery.

"Look out!" a trooper suddenly cried. "That brute is coming back to life!"

True enough, the grizzly had raised its head and spread its jaws. But it was the last heave of its mighty lungs, the last beat of its gigantic heart. Voicing a snarl of defiance at the puny humans who had brought him low, the grizzly exhaled loudly, then slumped, a lifeless husk.

Lieutenant Jacobson walked over and poked it with his sword, eliciting no response. "It's done for," he announced.

Sobbing drew Fargo around to find Professor Williams doubled over, raining tears. Going to her, he slid an arm around her shoulders. Hester voiced a muffled sob and clung to him, pressing her face against his buckskin shirt. The first sob brought on more. It was as if an inner dam had ruptured. She spewed tears in a torrent, crying until she had no more tears left to shed. His shirt became soaked.

"It was awful," Hester croaked in torment. "The single most horrible sight I've ever seen."

"Stay out here long enough and you'll see more," Fargo said. "The wilderness isn't for greenhorns or amateurs."

Sniffling, Hester raised her damp eyes to his. "I'm beginning to see that. I thought of it as a pristine wonderland filled with harmless, innocent creatures. Maybe I need to rethink my outlook."

Fargo nodded at Upton's body. "In more ways than one. If your friend had been holding a rifle instead of a pencil, he might still be alive. A knife wouldn't have done it. Or a lance or a bow." He mustered a grim smile. "Guns can come in handy after all."

"I suppose," she reluctantly admitted.

"Always remember, Professor. It isn't the weapon that's good or bad. It's the person who uses it." Fargo gazed thoughtfully across the prairie. "If white men and the Indians had it in them to get along peaceably, it wouldn't matter what kind of weapons they favored. But there are people on both sides who hate just for the sake of hating. Whites who think the only good Indian is a dead Indian. Indians who think the same about whites. They'll kill with whatever is handy. Guns. Clubs. Rocks."

Hester had regained some of her composure. Straightening, she wiped a sleeve across her face. "I'm sorry, Mr. Fargo. You're not the buffoon I mistook you for. I don't know how I can ever make amends. Please forgive me."

"Nothing to forgive." Fargo rotated, and saw Diane Marsten standing over the body, her face as pale as chalk. He had forgotten about her in all the excitement. Stepping in front of the corpse to block her view, he said, "Why torture yourself? We'll take care of burying him."

"So fragile," Diane whispered.

"What?"

"Our lives. They're so fragile. We're here one minute, gone the next." Diane shook as if an icy breeze had stroked her spine, then clasped her arms to her bosom. "Just a short while ago Clark was whistling and smiling and happy. Now look at him."

"Don't think about it," Fargo said.

"But I want to." Diane looked at him. "I don't want to ever forget this day. It's taught me an important lesson, perhaps the most important lesson of my life." She shivered again, so Fargo did with her as he had done with Hester. Diane snuggled against his side, her arms as frigid as ice. "I'm never taking a single moment for granted again. From here on out, I'm living life to the fullest."

"That's nice." What else could Fargo say? The woman had a knack for making more of things than they were. He'd met some like her before. People who had the misguided notion they were the most important things in all creation. Everything that took place had to have some bearing on their lives. Everything was an omen, or a sign, or a lesson to be learned. It never occurred to them that sometimes events just *happened*.

"Thank you for trying to save him," Diane said, her mouth almost brushing his chin. "It was very brave of you to go out there like you did. I'll never forget it."

Fargo shrugged. He had just done what needed doing.

"I mean it," Diane said, leaning closer. Her chest briefly rubbed against his, her warm breath caressing his cheek. Then she pulled back and lowered her arms. "We'll talk more later. I'm fine now, thank you."

The burial delayed them another hour. Jacobson had his men dig the grave. Bitterroot John wrapped Clark Upton in a spare blanket, and the body was solemnly lowered into the ground. Troopers filled in the hole. Hester had gathered flowers, which she arranged on top. Diane Marsten surprised Fargo by fashioning a crude cross and inserting it at the head of the dirt mound. "A few words should be said," she mentioned.

No one volunteered. Ringed around the grave, they self-consciously glanced at one another, each wanting the other to be the one to do it. Clearing his throat, Lieutenant Jacobson moved forward. "None of us are what you could call regular churchgoers, but I remember something from my childhood that should do." He launched into a recital of the Twenty-third Psalm.

It was a sober party who resumed their trek northward. No one joked. No one laughed. No one sang. With one exception. Only Bitterroot John was unaffected by the naturalist's death. He hummed to himself the whole afternoon.

Along about two, Diane Marsten asked to halt the column. A theodolite was broken out and positioned on a low promontory to the west, within earshot of the wagons. Both women, Fargo observed, wore revolvers and carried rifles. It took another hour for them to complete the first step in their survey.

Fargo was unwilling to stop again until twilight shrouded the basin. Sentries were posted, coffee was made. Fargo endeared himself to the soldiers by shooting an antelope, an exceptional shot from a hundred and fifty yards off. Fresh meat was a rare treat for them, and the boys in blue tore into the roasted chunks with relish.

Afterward, some of the troopers played cards while others wrote letters or simply relaxed. Lieutenant Jacobson cleaned his revolver. Bitterroot John was kept busy washing dishes and tending to the teams. The women lounged near the crackling fire.

Fargo joined them after making a circuit of the perimeter of the camp to verify everything was in order. A multitude of stars blazed in the heavens. From the northwest wafted a cool breeze. Now and again coyotes would yip, wolves would howl. It was a typical night in the wild, a night such as Fargo had experienced countless times. But the women were tremendously impressed.

"How incredible the sky is!" Hester marveled. "I've never seen so many stars before." She jabbed a finger at a streak of light to the southeast. "Oh, look! A meteor! My grandmother used to tell me that if you make a wish on a falling star, the wish always comes true."

Diane Marsten watched the streak fade. "My grandfather told me a falling star is God's snot. It shoots out of his nose when he sneezes."

Hester had tipped a cup to her mouth to sip coffee. Bursting into peals of mirth, she spilled some on her pants and jumped up, shaking her shapely leg. "Owwww! It's hot enough to scald me!"

The troopers cackled. Bitterroot John slapped his side and brayed like a mule. Fargo joined in the mirth, too, enjoying a rare belly laugh.

"What an awful thing to say," Hester scolded Diane. "What kind of man was your grandfather, anyway?"

"A regular character," Diane said. "The black sheep of the Marsten family. He had been a sailor in his younger days and visited most of the major ports. The tales he could tell!" She smiled dreamily. "He pretended to be a rascal, but at heart he was a kitten."

Fargo poured some coffee for himself and sat back. He was pleased to see the women let down their hair, as it were, and stop acting so high and mighty. When they weren't trying to impress everyone with how smart they were, they were nice as could be.

The talk turned to their childhoods. Fargo gathered that Hester had been pampered rotten, her parents being wealthy enough to afford to send her to the best schools and dress her in the most expensive clothes. Diane had a harder time of it. She'd had to scrape and struggle for every dollar, and had made her way to college largely through her own efforts. "I've never had to depend on anyone other than myself," she remarked. "And that's how I like it." She paused. "I don't think I could depend on someone else. I wouldn't know how."

The soldiers turned in early. Two men were left on guard duty with instructions to wake their reliefs in three hours. Bitterroot John wrapped himself in a blanket under a wagon and was soon snoring loud enough to be heard clear back at Fort Bridger. The women were the last to retire.

Fargo finished his fourth cup of coffee, and rose. As their guide, their safety was his responsibility. He made another circuit of the camp before calling it a day, stopping to spend a few moments with the Ovaro and listen to the chorus of night sounds. No other campfires flared in the vastness of the night, an encouraging sign. Giving the stallion a last pat, he swiveled to go back. And saw an inky shape glide toward him.

"You're still up, Skye?" Diane Marsten whispered. "I can't sleep. What's your excuse?" She had thrown her blanket over her shoulders, and her golden locks cascaded over it in lustrous profusion.

"I was just about to bed down," Fargo disclosed.

"Care to go for a stroll? I could use a little exercise. It will help me get to sleep." Diane gently grasped his hand and steered him toward a small cluster of trees some forty feet distant. Whether by accident or design, she slipped from camp at a point where neither of the sentries was liable to spot them.

Fargo did not object. Thanks to the coffee he was wide awake. And if she had in mind what he *thought* she had in mind, well, it was fine by him. She must have splashed on more perfume because the sweet fragrance was stronger than it had been. Her palm was soft and warm to the touch. He liked how the blanket swung seductively from side to side with every step she took.

"I've always liked a long walk before bedtime," Diane whispered. "Helps calm the nerves after a hectic day. Plus, it's beneficial to the constitution."

"There you go again with the big words."

"Old habits are hard to break. Not that it would pay for me to break this one. My colleagues at Albany believe verbal skills and intellect go hand in hand. They claim a large vocabulary is a sign of a large brain."

"How about large breasts?"

They were close to the trees. Diane abruptly stopped and faced him, her face inscrutable in the darkness. "I beg your pardon?" she said huskily. "What do large breasts have to do with anything?"

"If you were to ask most men which they like best in a woman, a large brain or large breasts, guess which they would pick?" Fargo moved closer. "I'll show you why." Audaciously, he cupped her glorious mounds. She tensed, her hand rising as if to hit him. For a second he thought she actually might. Then her body melted against his and the blanket fell to the ground. Her mouth hungrily sought his lips. She was soft and yielding, her tongue velvety smooth. Kissing her was like sucking on hard candy. Sweet, delicious, wonderful.

A fluttering sigh escaped her as Fargo tweaked a hardening nipple through her shirt. Her nails found his shoulders and dug in deep. She sagged, as if she had gone weak in the legs. Sweeping her into his arms, he carried her into the trees and set her down in a little starlit glade. With her luxurious hair and swelling chest, her long legs and limpid eyes, she was exquisitely lovely.

"You must think my behavior is terribly brazen," Diane said. "But please don't think ill of me. I'm not a wanton hussy. I just—"

Fargo put a finger to her lips. "Do us both a favor and keep quiet. For once in your life, just enjoy yourself. Don't talk us to death." To smother her response, he latched his mouth on to hers and probed his tongue between her parted teeth. His right hand covered her breast and he squeezed just hard enough to cause her to squirm and coo.

Diane heeded his advice. She did not chatter aimlessly. She did not try to analyze every moment. She gave herself to him in total abandon, her vibrant body an oven waiting to be stoked.

Undoing her shirt with its many buttons was a chore. She gasped when the night air struck her naked skin, then gasped again when his hand was applied to her bare bosom. Her nipple was a nail, her breast engorged and fit to burst. Lowering his head, he lathered every square inch of both globes while kneading her belly and thighs. Her pants slid loosely down over her hips once he had undone her belt.

"Ohhhhhhh," Diane moaned.

Fargo kissed her neck, her ears, her earlobes. She was particularly sensitive there, and would not stop wriggling and sighing. When he sucked on a lobe, she arched her spine and clawed his back, her legs pumping. She was as hungry for him as the soldiers had been for the antelope. No, more so, since Fargo had the impression she hadn't given herself to a man in a long while.

Diane grew more animated as the minutes languidly flitted by. She stripped off his hat and his shirt. Her mouth sought his throat, his chest. When he dipped a hand between her legs to massage her inner thighs, she went rigid for a few moments, her rosy lips wide in pure carnal joy. Then her hands swooped to his pants and tugged at them as if to tear them off. He had to help by unfastening his gunbelt.

Excitedly, Diane pushed the pants down around his knees, freeing his rock-hard organ. Gingerly, almost fearfully, she touched him, her fingers tracing delicate lines up and down his member. She pulled back to stare at it, her eyelids hooded, lust oozing from every pore. "So big. So solid."

Fargo clamped his mouth to hers. He felt her fingers wrap around his pole, felt her lightly stroke him. A constriction formed in his throat. His pulse raced. Instinctively, she knew just what to do to bring him to the brink. As it was, he had to struggle to keep from erupting too soon.

Easing her flat onto her back, Fargo stretched out, his chest against those swollen hills. His right hand slid along the flat of her abdomen to the bushy junction of her creamy thighs. Her bottom scooted upward in a pumping cadence, hinting at her own overwhelming desire for release.

Fargo dropped a hand to her womanhood. The suddenness of it made her suck in a breath. Her legs trembled. He rubbed a finger along her slit to the tiny knob at its peak. At the first contact, Diane tossed her head and uttered a low cry. She was lost in sensual rapture. He, though, did not forget where they were. The whole time, in the back of his mind, a tiny part of him took note of everything that went on around them. The rustling of the trees, the nicker of a horse in camp, the lonesome wail of a roving wolf, he heard them all.

Suddenly Fargo sensed something else. He could not say how or why he knew, but as surely as he was lying there half naked with his pistol out of ready reach, he knew that they were not alone. Someone—or something—was watching them.

# 6

Skye Fargo nuzzled Diane Marsten's breasts. In doing so, he tilted his head high enough to see the surrounding vegetation. There was little undergrowth, mostly saplings and a few older trees including a majestic willow. Diane continued to "Ooh!" and "Aah!" and writhe in erotic delight as he rolled a nipple with his tongue while swiveling from side to side so he could see behind them.

Nothing moved. But Fargo didn't doubt his instincts. They had served him well time and time again. Nor was he alone in that regard. Most frontiersmen developed a sort of sixth sense without being aware they were doing so. Many Indians had it, too.

Life in the raw was responsible. A man never knew from one day to the next whether he would be alive to see the next dawn. The threat of danger, of abrupt, violent death, was almost constant. Small wonder that men and women who had to endure that constant threat somehow refined an inner sense that alerted them when danger was near.

Fargo switched to the professor's other breast. She was sighing contentedly, her hands in his hair, her glazed eyes fixed on the patch of sky directly above. Without being obvious, he scoured the trees again. This time he found what he was looking for.

The base of the willow was much wider than it should be low down to the ground. It bulged, as if a large knob protruded from the trunk. Peering closely, Fargo saw that the knob had definite rounded contours. Exactly the contours, say, of someone kneeling there and spying on them.

The big question was whether the skulker was friendly or hostile. Fargo would not put it past one of the sentries to have noticed their departure and shadowed them to see what they were up to. Then again, Jacobson struck him as being a stickler for discipline, and no trooper in his right mind courted a week in the guardhouse, or worse.

So if not a soldier, then who? Bitterroot John had been sawing logs. Hester had been sound asleep, too. Was it an Indian? Maybe a warrior who had been spying on the camp? Fargo twisted again, to the left. His Colt was lying just beyond his reach. If he grabbed for it, the man behind the tree was bound to catch on that he had been seen.

Fargo had another idea. Clutching Diane to him in an apparent fit of passion, he rolled her to the left, ending up close enough to the Colt to snatch it quickly if he had to. She moaned and raked his back with her sharp nails, drawing blood, her thighs opening and closing with each stroke of his forefinger. At least one of them was enjoying the moment.

Fargo glanced at the willow again. The silhouette was still there but it had moved, exposing more of the lurker. He thought he saw a mane of hair hanging to the shoulders. The person moved, confirming it, and giving him a clue to the watcher's identity.

It had to be Hester Williams. She must have woken up just as they left and trailed after them. For a woman born with a silver spoon in her mouth, a woman to whom breeding and cultured conduct were everything, her manners left a lot to be desired. Maybe she was one of those who got excited watching others make love. Or maybe she was simply curious.

Inwardly, Fargo smiled. Whatever her reason for spying on them, he was not going to stop just because she was there. Forgetting about her for the time being, he kneeled between Diane's silken legs. Her hand enfolded his redwood, and tugged.

"Please, Skye. Please."

Fargo aligned the tip, gripped her hips, and thrust into her as if he were trying to impale her clear to her throat. Diane's whole body seemed to rise up off the ground. Her eyes grew as big around as saucers, and for a few moments she stopped breathing. Then, in convulsive abandon, she glued herself to him and thrust her posterior in a steady frantic cadence. She was over the brink. He felt her gush, felt her stomach heave, felt her breasts mash against his chest. She pumped and pumped until, voicing a strangled cry, she thrashed like a madwoman and then suddenly sagged, spent.

Fargo wasn't done, however. He continued to stroke, rocking on his knees. Her eyes widened again and she looked at him strangely. Gradually, her hips began to move once more, matching his thrusts tit for tat. Lips as hot as red coals found his mouth and melted against his own.

Fargo let the release come slowly. He rocked and rocked, the sensation of undiluted pleasure spreading throughout his body. It grew more and more intense. So intense, it was like trying to hold back an explosion *after* the keg of black powder had gone off. It just couldn't be done. The spark came when Diane reached down to cup his jewels. He erupted. His head swam, his vision spun, a thousand dazzling pinpoints of light danced in front of him. He spurted like a geyser, spurted until he was spent.

Exhausted, slick with perspiration, Fargo sagged on top of Diane. Her pillowy mounds cushioned him. Another glance at the tree showed Hester was gone. Grinning, Fargo eased onto his side and lay quietly, relishing the all too rare moment of absolute serenity. Without meaning to, he dozed.

When Fargo awoke, an hour or more had gone by, judging by the positions of the stars. Diane slept soundly, an arm across his shoulder. Gently removing it, he sat up and pulled his pants back on. Reclaiming his gunbelt was next, then his hat. Quietly, he rose and padded to the willow. It was doubtful he would find anything, but he had an urge to look. Thick grass eliminated the likelihood of there being any prints. He sniffed, thinking he would register Hester's perfume, but instead he smelled an oily scent that puzzled him until its true nature hit him with the force of a physical blow.

It wasn't oil. It was the scent of bear grease. Indians sometimes used the grease to slick their hair. Which meant that the person who had been spying on them had not been Hester Williams at all. It had been a warrior. Maybe a hostile warrior.

A cold chill gripped him, and Fargo frowned. He had blundered badly. It might have cost them their lives. He surveyed the trees but the Indian was long gone. In the morning he would return and look for tracks. In the meantime, it was best to get Diane to camp and warn the soldiers trouble might be on their horizon.

Diane Marsten did not want to wake up. Fargo shook her lightly and all she did was smack her lips and mutter, "Too tired. Too tired." When he shook harder, she slapped his arm, mumbling, "Leave me alone." He tried a third time, eliciting, "Please, Jim. I just want to sleep."

Who was Jim? Fargo gripped her elbow and jerked. "Diane," he said loudly. "We have to get back."

"What? Who?" Her eyes blinked and she sluggishly sought to sit up but couldn't. Fargo gave her a hand, holding her steady while she collected her wits. "Where are we?" she asked in a daze, then looked down at herself and jumped as if bitten by a rattler. "Oh my! I forgot!" She glanced sheepishly at him. "You're dressed already? Is anything wrong?"

"No," Fargo fibbed. "But it's late. We should get back before anyone notices we're missing. Jacobson might send some soldiers to find us."

That spurred her into moving quickly. She shyly turned her back to him while she dressed. He did not bother to point out that he had seen all there was to see of her, or mention she had nothing to be embarrassed about. Most women tended to do the same, and nothing a man said would get them to change. As a dove in a dance hall had once put it, "Women aren't as crude as men. We're more private about our thoughts and feelings. And our bodies."

The wind had picked up, as it usually did at night in open country. Fargo held her by one hand and rested his other on the Colt as they threaded through the saplings. They retrieved her blanket.

The camp lay silent under the stars. A sentry was over by the horses, his back to them. The other guard was across the camp, pacing. The fire was still going but it had been allowed to burn low.

Neither of the troopers challenged them. Fargo realized a warrior could crawl right into camp without being seen. It was not a comforting thought. He led her over near Hester, who did not stir. Diane pecked him on the cheek and whispered, "Thank you!" into his ear, and lay down.

Before turning in, Fargo visited with each of the sentries, asking if they had seen or heard anything out of the ordinary. They hadn't. Both were young recruits, and their inexperience was an invitation to disaster. The second one he approached, the youngest, gave a little cough after he warned about Indians being in the area.

"Mind if I ask you a question, sir?"

Fargo looked at him.

"Aren't you ever—?" the trooper paused uncertainly.

"Out with it."

Nodding, the youngster asked, "Aren't you ever afraid out here? I mean, isn't it scary knowing there are Indians and bears and the like all over the place? That what happened to Mr. Upton could just as well happen to you?"

"Upton was an idiot. Keep your eyes skinned and your guns loaded and you won't wind up like him." Fargo had met plenty of troopers just like this one, men so green behind the ears you'd swear they had grass on their heads instead of hair. "Where are you from, Private?"

"Jessup, sir. Private Jessup. I'm from Ohio. My father is a baker. He wasn't very happy when I decided to enlist. But I wanted a little excitement in my life. I wanted to see the West, and a stint in the military seemed the best way."

"Plan to go back there again one day, do you?"

"Yes, sir. I figure to take over my father's business when he gets older." Jessup nervously gazed into the murky gloom. "To be honest, army life isn't all I thought it would be. Instead of excitement, I spend most of my time scrubbing and cleaning and drilling until my feet are ready to fall off."

Fargo did not mince words. "Only a jackass goes looking for excitement when it might cost his life." The boy shriveled like a wilted flower. Taking pity on him, Fargo said, "If you want to live long enough to see your folks again, take some advice. When you're on guard duty, don't move around any more than you have to. Don't make noise. Crouch down every now and then so you can see if anyone is sneaking up on you. And whatever you do, don't look at the fire."

"Why not?"

"Because it takes time for your eyes to adjust when you look away again. For about half a minute you're as blind as a bat. And Indians know it. An Apache would slit your throat before you could blink."

Jessup gulped. "The other fellas were saying that you've fought every kind of Indian there is. Comanches, Blackfeet, you name it. How'd you survive all this time?"

"By never taking anything for granted."

Fargo had not appreciated how tired he was until he spread out under a blanket with his saddle for a pillow. It was a little past midnight. He figured he would fall asleep right away but the skulker in the trees had his nerves on edge. He tossed and turned until one or so.

The clatter of a coffeepot woke Fargo shortly after first light. One of the troopers was making coffee. Jacobson was combing his hair. Bitterroot John had gone to the river for water and was bearing a bucket into camp. The women were sound asleep.

Fargo sought out the officer after breakfast, which consisted of leftover antelope, wolfed cold. Without mentioning Diane Marsten's part in the previous night's activities, he reported seeing the figure in the trees.

"You should have mentioned this sooner," the lieutenant said. "What if it's a war party? If they had jumped us in the middle of the night?"

"I told the guards," Fargo said. "And Indians rarely attack after dark." He excused himself to go check for tracks.

A carpet of thick grass thwarted him. Fargo ranged around the willow in ever-widening circles but did not discover so much as a scuff mark. He was south of the stand and about to head back when a single print caught his eye. It was the sole of a moccasin, etched in hard-packed dirt. The outline was not very clear, but if Fargo had to hazard a guess, he would say the owner of the moccasin was a Ute.

It did not bode well. The surveyors were no longer in Ute country. Any bands roving north of Fort Bridger were more than likely war parties, either out to raid the Shoshones or the Flatheads, or on their way home after a raid.

Lieutenant Jacobson split his men. Only half now rode behind the wagon. Four rode in front, and two troopers were to either side. No one could get at the wagons, and the women, without going through the soldiers.

Fargo was on the lookout for more sign. Often he saw deer and elk tracks, bear and cougar, coyote and wolf. Twice he came on ground badly trampled by buffalo. But no human spoor. Toward the middle of the morning, while the professors were taking measurements, Fargo circled to the rear to catch any pursuers by surprise. But no one was there. He crisscrossed the grassland bordering the Green River without result.

Two explanations were possible. Either the warrior had been alone, which was highly unlikely, or the war party was taking special pains to avoid being seen until the warriors were ready to strike.

Fargo mentioned it to Jacobson. The officer insisted that from then on the women must not go anywhere without a pair of troopers along. Diane agreed but Hester balked. She was big enough to take care of herself, she told him. It went in one ear and out the other. Jacobson would not change his policy.

The next day passed in similar fashion. Several times Fargo roved wide of the column. All he stumbled on were prairie dogs, ferrets and grouse.

By the end of the fourth day Fargo began to think they were safe. Hostiles intending to attack would have done so already. That evening the soldiers held a little celebration for Private Jessup, who had turned nineteen. Bitterroot John baked small cakes in honor of the occasion in the portable stove.

The next sunrise was brisk and clear. Fargo helped hitch the teams. When they were underway, he rode alongside Lieutenant

Jacobson. Neither of the professors had said anything about having the soldiers return to the post. After what had happened to Upton, they were glad to have the troopers along.

Presently the Green River angled to the northeast, overlooked by a bluff to the west. Not half an hour later, as Fargo idly scanned the countryside, sunlight flashed on the bluff's rim. "We're not alone anymore," he casually revealed.

Jacobson's head snapped up. "Indians? You've spotted them?"

"On the bluff. Keep riding as if we don't have a care in the world. The next move is theirs."

The lieutenant shifted anxiously. "I disagree. We should find a defensible position and dig in until their intentions are made known."

"Do that and they'll attack for sure. The only reason they've held off this long is because they think we're too stupid to know they're out there." Fargo pretended to stretch while raking the bluff from north to south. "If they don't hit us by noon, I'll try to swing on around them."

The hours dragged by, the temperature climbed. Insects droned nonstop. The clomp of hooves, the creaking and rattling of the wagons, the clatter of accouterments lulled the soldiers into being drowsy. Jacobson spread word down the line for everyone to keep alert. From then on, the soldiers rode with their rifles across their thighs, ready for action.

Noontime arrived. At a junction with a tributary, a narrow creek that wound to the northwest, Fargo called a halt. Open terrain on three sides safeguarded their flanks. To their right was a gully into which they could retreat if pressed.

To give the impression they were going on about their regular routine, Fargo had the professors lug out their theodolite. Bitterroot John got a fire going and set on a coffeepot. The soldiers spread out, trying to make it look as if they were lounging around. But a closer look disclosed they kept their weapons handy and did little talking.

"I won't be long," Fargo said as he forked leather. "If you hear shots, fall back into the gully and set up skirmish lines."

"You're welcome to take a couple of the men with you," Jacobson offered.

Fargo shook his head. "If the worst comes to pass, you'll need them more than I will." Wheeling the pinto, he trotted along the tributary, following the stream to where it skirted the north side of the bluff. In the distance were mountains shimmering jade green in the heat of the day. Unlimbering the Henry, he levered a round into the chamber and climbed.

Short of the top, Fargo dismounted and advanced. Mesquite and scrub brush met his gaze. Not Indians. When he was convinced it was safe, he climbed back on the stallion and prowled southward along the flat summit. Sooner or later he would find what he was looking for. The junction was still out of sight when he reined up next to a sheer drop of some sixty feet. Another half a mile and he should be at the spot where the flash had come from.

Suddenly popping sounds reached his ears. It sounded like firecrackers but Fargo knew better. Cursing, he hauled on the reins, backtracking to a game trail that wound to the bottom. He flew down it at a breakneck pace, not caring about the risk, and raced for the junction of the stream and the Green River.

A spur hid it from view. Only after he passed the spur did he see puffs and swirls of gunsmoke rising above the battle site. Faint war whoops and jumbled shouts inspired him to go faster.

Fargo was still a quarter of a mile away when the firing ended. A few last whoops were heard, then ominous silence. Galloping on until he was a hundred yards out, he slowed to take stock of the situation. Smoke hung thick in the air now. It roiled upward from one of the wagons, which had been set ablaze. He slowed when he was within a hundred yards. Looping the reins over around his left wrist, he jammed the Henry to his shoulder.

There was no sign of movement anywhere. A couple of blue-clad bodies lay near the river, another figure was near the wagons, four more near the mouth of the gully. Two dead horses added to the scene of slaughter. The rest of the mounts and the teams to the wagons were gone.

Dreading the worst, Fargo warily approached. The ground around the camp had been churned by unshod hooves. He saw feathered shafts jutting from both wagons. Arrows also protruded from the bodies of the two dead soldiers who lay in spreading scarlet pools next to the Green River. The dead man close to the burning wagon wasn't a trooper, though. A slug had added a new nostril to the face of a young Ute warrior.

The tracks told Fargo a lot. Some of the troopers had been at the river when the Utes swept down on them from out of a cleft in the bluff. Firing as they retreated, the soldiers had regrouped around the wagons, only to be driven back. Their trail led into the gully. The Indians had gone to the northeast along the bank of the Green. Where they were now was anybody's guess, but Fargo doubted they had gone very far.

Reining toward the gully, Fargo discovered that two of the four who had fallen there were soldiers. The other pair were Utes, cut down in a withering hail of lead. Jacobson and his men had put up stiff resistance.

"Lieutenant?" Fargo hollered, and the next instant instinctively ducked as a rifle banged and lead sizzled past his head. "Hold on!" he bellowed. "It's me, Fargo!"

Shouts rose. The officer was berating someone for firing without permission. Then Jacobson appeared, holding his revolver and beckoning. "Hurry up! They're out there somewhere. And they got hold of some of our guns."

Fargo quickly trotted on by and slid from the saddle. The eight remaining soldiers, both professors and Bitterroot John were all there. Two of the troopers were wounded, being tended by the women. The rest lined the rim of the gully, three on each side. Private Jessup was one of them, and he shot Fargo a nervous smile.

"We held them, Mr. Fargo! By God, we held them!"

Lieutenant Jacobson had backed into the gully. "Eyes front, Private," he barked. "Those red devils will try something else now that their first attack failed." He wiped his perspiring brow with a sleeve. "How we lived through it, I'll never know. They were on us so quickly, it's a wonder any of us are alive."

"Tell me what happened," Fargo coaxed. The officer was as

tense as a steel spring. Talking would help calm his jagged nerves.

Jacobson licked his lips. "They must have been watching and waiting for just the right moment. I had ordered half the detail to take their horses to the river for a drink. The rest of us were taking it easy. Since there had been no sign of the hostiles, I assumed we were safe enough." Jacobson paused. "Was I ever wrong."

"Go on," Fargo said when the officer clammed up.

"They came at us out of that cleft yonder." Jacobson pointed. "It doesn't look wide enough for riders to get through, does it? But those savages did. They were at the river before we got off a shot. Two of the water detail dropped in a rain of arrows. The rest fell back." Jacobson took a deep breath. When he resumed, his voice had lost its strained quality. "We formed up around the wagons and tried to hold the heathens off. What with all the racket, most of our horses bolted. When I saw that we couldn't hold out there very long, I fell back to the gully as you had recommended. The Indians tried to stop us but we made it."

Fargo moved to the mouth and gazed along the Green. The warriors were probably spying on him at that very moment but he could not see them. Their next attack would be executed with supreme stealth. Or they might be content to lie out there and pick off the troopers if the boys in blue tried to go anywhere. Why they had let him ride in was a mystery.

Jacobson materialized. "Don't tell the men this, but I was never so afraid in all my life. I've only been in one other engagement. A few Sioux attacked a supply column I was with. Some shots were swapped, but that was the extent of it."

"You did just fine," Fargo said. He coughed when the breeze shifted, swirling smoke into the gully. The first wagon was being devoured by hungry flames. Thankfully, the second one was parked far enough from the first that there was little chance of it igniting.

"Are they Utes, like you thought?"

Fargo nodded while gauging their prospects. Four dead, two wounded. No horses other than his own. And the wagon which held their food would soon be reduced to ashes. It did not look good.

"What will they do next?"

"There's no telling," Fargo answered, and almost as if on cue, three warriors appeared on horseback, walking their mounts from out of a cluster of cottonwoods across the stream. They held up their hands to show they were not holding weapons, then started to cross. In the center was a tall Ute on a splendid bay, a warrior who wore a bright red headband. "I'll be damned," Fargo said to himself.

"Red Band!" Lieutenant Jacobson cried, extending his revolver. "That renegade! I should have known!"

"No. Don't." Fargo grabbed the officer's wrist. "They want to talk. Let's hear what they have to say."

Jacobson tried to pull free but could not match Fargo's strength. "Why bother?" he said. "They're not about to let us leave here alive. We should kill him while we can. Maybe the rest will leave us be."

"It doesn't work that way," Fargo said. Slaying Red Band would only incite the others to a fever pitch of vengeful bloodlust. "Order your men not to shoot unless I say so."

Glowering, Jacobson complied. The three Utes calmly came closer. At a signal from Red Band the other two halted. Their leader proceeded to within a few feet of where Fargo and the officer stood. He gave the lieutenant a glance of utter contempt, then nodded at Fargo. "We meet again, white-eye."

"Speak what is on your mind," Fargo said.

"Same as before. I want woman." Red Band's mouth quirked upward. "This time you have some, eh?"

Lieutenant Jacobson could not contain himself. "Forget it, you bastard! The only way you're getting your hands on those ladies is over our dead bodies!"

Red Band bent forward and grinned in outright spite. "That be fine, soldier dog. That be just fine. Give woman or all soldiers die."

# 7

Lieutenant Jacobson had a temper. In a civilian it would be bad enough, but in a professional military man, someone whose judgment others depended on for their very lives, it was a flaw that could have disastrous consequences.

Skye Fargo was not caught napping when Jacobson suddenly lunged and tried to seize hold of Red Band's leg. Letting the Henry drop, he sprang between them, gripping the officer by the collar while simultaneously preventing Jacobson from snapping off a shot. "This is not the time."

"Let go of me!" Jacobson raged. "You have no right! I'll report this to Major Canby when we get back."

"Go right ahead." Fargo glanced at the Ute. "Anything else? If not, skeddaddle. And think about the mistake you're making."

Red Band straightened. "You be smart, white man. Not like bluecoat." He sneered at Jacobson. "I go now. Let you think. When sun is there—he indicated at a position in the sky—I come back. Maybe give woman then." The warrior began to turn the bay, then paused. "Wait. What mistake?"

"I've heard the story," Fargo said. "I know why you're doing this. And you're wrong." He released the officer, who had quieted but was fit to explode at the slightest provocation. "The doctor at the fort did everything he could for Morning Dove. Blaming all whites for her death is wrong. Trying to steal a white woman to make up for her loss is wrong."

"Not your wife who die," Red Band said bitterly.

"Even your own medicine couldn't cure her. So why blame the whites?"

Red Band made a slashing motion with his hand. "Trappers say white medicine strong. Traders say white medicine strong. Man who speak of Father in sky say white medicine strong." He snorted. "So when wife be sick, I take her to fort. What happen? She die. Prove white men liars. Prove white medicine not strong."

"But why take a white woman to make up for Morning Dove's loss?" Fargo persisted. "Haven't you heard they make terrible wives?" Which was true, as far as it went. Many Indians were of the opinion that white women were too weak, too soft and too lazy. A Kiowa he knew had once joked it would be better to live with a cat than a white woman because cats did not whine and cry all the time.

Red Band was unfazed. "Whites take my woman. I take white woman."

It would be pointless to argue. But Fargo gave it one last try. "There must be quite a few Ute women who would be happy to come live in your lodge. Go back to your village, Red Band. Pick one of them. Live a long, happy life. Forget this loco notion."

"I want white woman."

"Then we've said all we need to."

The tall Ute grunted. "I be wrong before. You speak with straight tongue." He turned the bay, adding over a shoulder. "I almost be sorry I must kill you. But not others. Bluecoats all die soon unless give woman."

Lieutenant Jacobson was itching to squeeze the trigger. His whole body shook and his lips were compressed into thin slits. "I should do it now," he growled. "I should shoot the son of a bitch before he's out of range."

"In the back?" Fargo countered. He didn't move into the gully until after the three Utes had recrossed the stream. Jacobson glared, then jammed the revolver into his holster. Shouldering past, Fargo mulled his options. The troopers on the rim were crouched low. Their wounded companions were resting.

Bitterroot John had sidled near to the opening. "I heard what went on. Are you an Injun lover, mister? The lieutenant was right. You should have blown out that buck's wick while you could."

Diane Marsten and Hester Williams hurried over. "One of the men has a wound in the thigh, the other in the arm," the former reported. "Neither is life-threatening, but they won't be able to move around much for a while."

"They might not have a choice," Fargo noted.

"Do you have a plan to get us out of this mess?" Hester asked. "How can we go anywhere with only one horse? I'm no expert, but I don't think we would last very long on foot with those Indians hovering over us."

"We wouldn't," Lieutenant Jacobson declared with a resentful stare at the Trailsman. "I won't try to deceive you, ladies. Our prospects are grim. We have no food, no water. All the Utes have to do is wait us out. When we get thirsty enough, we'll try for the river and they'll drop us like flies."

Diane was appalled. "Is that all we'll do? Sit here twiddling our thumbs for days on end, growing weaker and weaker, until we're simply too weak to fight back?"

"No." The kernel of a plan had taken shape in Fargo's mind. "Did anyone see what happened to the horses and the teams?"

"I told you. They bolted," Jacobson said.

"Did you see them run off with your own eyes?" Fargo inquired. The answer was crucial to the success of his scheme.

"Yes," the lieutenant said, then blinked. "Well, no, actually. I saw them mill around and heard them whinny. I think I saw some trot northward. But I didn't pay a lot of attention. I had other things on my mind, such as keeping my men alive."

Commendable, Fargo reflected, but a wise officer would safeguard the mounts his men relied on for their survival just as vigorously as he looked out for the welfare of the men themselves. Fargo did not say as much, though. It would be rubbing salt on an open wound, as it were. Jacobson was already mad enough.

"Why do you want to know?"

Fargo stepped to the side of the gully. "The only thing warriors like more than counting coup is adding to their horse herds."

"So you think the Utes have them? That our animals must be close by?" Diane asked.

"Close enough for me to slip out at sunset and bring them back," Fargo proposed.

Preposterous," Lieutenant Jacobson said. "There must be twelve or thirteen warriors left. Your hair will wind up on a lodge pole."

"It's my hair," Fargo could not resist saying. Climbing, he removed his hat. Private Jessup was on his right, studying him. "Seen any sign of our horses?"

"No, sir. I sure haven't."

Nor were they likely to. Fargo was sure the Utes had stashed the animals well out of sight, but not so far off that the warriors couldn't reclaim them in a hurry should it be necessary. The best bet was somewhere along the river, somewhere the trees were as thick as fleas on an old coon dog. Approximately half a mile up the Green was a particularly heavy belt of vegetation. An ideal spot.

"I shot one," Private Jessup mentioned. "When they tried to cut us off from the gully, I brought one down with a single shot."

"Feel proud, do you?" Fargo was more interested in memorizing the best route to the spot where their animals might be.

"At first I did. But then I got to thinking. I broke one of the Ten Commandments. 'Thou shalt not kill,' it says. And I went and killed someone. So what if it was an Indian? I don't think that makes much difference to the Almighty, do you?"

"Dead is dead."

Jessup nodded. "You know, I never really thought it would come to this. Thousands of guys serve their hitches and never fire a shot at an enemy. I always figured to be one of them."

"We all figure wrong sometimes." Fargo detected movement in a tree sixty yards away. Also in a patch of weeds half that distance up the stream.

"How do you deal with it?" Jessup asked.

"With what?"

"Killing. What else?"

"I don't think about it," Fargo replied. He never had. When

86

it had to be done, he did it, and he didn't spend time afterward moaning and groaning about what an awful person he must be for having taken a life. He wasn't a coldhearted killer like some he had met. He only killed in self-defense or in the defense of others.

"You don't?" Trooper Jessup said. "We must not be much alike, then. It's all I've been thinking about since I pulled the trigger."

"Keep your mind on the Utes or you won't have anything to think about ever again. You'll be dead." Fargo slid down the incline. On the opposite rim Lieutenant Jacobson was speaking to one of the men. Diane tended the wounded. Hester was at the mouth of the gully, engaged in an argument with Bitterroot John. They spoke in whispers but Fargo caught a few words. Enough to give him an idea what they were arguing about. He joined them.

Bitterroot John was the first to notice. "What the hell do you want, mister? We're havin' us a private talk. It's none of your business."

"It is when you're talking about riding to the fort for help," Fargo responded.

The scruffy jack-of-all-trades frowned. "What's wrong with that? It's only common sense. I could ride all day and all night and be at the fort by late tomorrow. A relief column could reach here by the day after if they pushed real hard."

Hester gestured. "Tell him not to go, Skye. It would be suicide. The Indians must have the gully completely surrounded by now. They'd see him. He wouldn't get a hundred feet, and I don't want him to throw his life away."

Fargo held the Henry low against his leg. "Don't worry. He's not going anywhere."

Bitterroot John shifted. "Why the hell not?"

"Because the only horse here is mine, and the only way you could get your hands on him would be to steal him." Suddenly jamming the Henry's muzzle against the man's groin, Fargo growled, *No one steals my stallion.*"

Bitterroot John started to swing the stock of his Sharps at Fargo's head but thought better of the notion. "Damn it! You act awful high-and-mighty, mister. One of us reachin' the fort is the only hope these ladies have. Red Band ain't about to give up until he gets his paws on one of 'em."

Fargo didn't remove the Henry. "By the time you reached Bridger, you'd be exhausted. You'd need a day just to rest up. Add two days or so for the soldiers to reach us. That's a total of five or six, twice what you claimed. By then it would be all over."

"Says you. Folks can go a week or better without food. I've done it myself a heap of times when pickin's were scarce out on the prairie. This bunch could hold out until the soldier boys arrived."

"Without food, yes. But not without water. Three days is about the limit." Fargo stepped back. "So you're not going anywhere. Not on my pinto. But since you're so eager to get out of here, you'll help me out tonight."

"You've lost me."

"When we leave, all of us are going together. To do that, we need the horses back."

Bitterroot John glanced at the north rim, then at Fargo. "You can't mean you're thinkin' of sneakin' on out there after dark to try and find 'em? Are you addlepated? Injuns are like ghosts. They'd slit our throats before we knew what was happening."

"You'd better hope they don't," Fargo said, smiling. "Because you're going, whether you want to or not."

"Like hell I am. You can't make me."

"Care to bet?" Fargo said, and drove the barrel of the Henry into Bitterroot John's gut. John doubled over, wheezing and spitting. Grasping the front of his homespun shirt, Fargo yanked him erect. "Who did you think you were fooling?" he grated. "You don't give a damn about the rest of us. All you're interested in is saving your own hide."

"Skye, don't!" Hester said.

Fargo gave John a shove that dumped him on his backside. "Be ready to go an hour after sunset. Give me any guff, and I'll drag you along by the ears." Pivoting, Fargo moved away, aware everyone in the gully was watching. Fingers snagged his arm, halting him.

"That was unspeakably rude," Professor Williams scolded. "There is no excuse for what you did. I insist you apologize to that poor man."

Fargo laughed coldly.

Incensed, Hester hauled off and slapped him. She was even more incensed when he immediately slapped her in return. Shaken, she pressed a hand to her red cheek and gaped at him as if he were some sort of monstrous fiend. "Well! We certainly had you pegged that first day, didn't we? You're nothing but an uncouth ruffian!"

"Is that a fact?" Fargo said, and let her have it with both verbal barrels. "Are you sure you went to college? I'm amazed you even know how to think. If you did, you'd realize the favor I just did you. And Diane."

Confusion crept into Hester's angry features. "What are you prattling about? You didn't do anything for us. All you were worried about is your stupid horse."

"Use that brain you're so proud of," Fargo said, tapping his own noggin. "Imagine what will happen if we can't find the other mounts."

"I already know. Those horrible Indians will keep us pinned down until they're ready to finish us off."

"Before it comes to that, we'll put Diane and you on the Ovaro. The stallion can handle the double weight. When the rest of us rush the Utes to keep them occupied, the two of you will slip out. It should work if we time it right."

Hester blinked. "That's the main reason you won't let John take him? Because it's the only hope Diane and I might have?"

"Pick whatever reason you like," Fargo said, and walked off to be by himself. He sat on the slope, positioned so the Ovaro was always in sight since he wouldn't put it past Bitterroot John to try and steal the pinto in broad daylight. Lying back, he propped his head on his arm. He needed to rest before nightfall. The crunch of footsteps told him he wouldn't have the opportunity.

"What on earth was that all about?" Diane Marsten asked. "I

saw you hit her, yet she just told me you're the most wonderful man alive."

"Keep an eye on Bitterroot John. He's up to no good."

"I can believe that. I never have trusted him. Being around him makes my skin crawl." Diane knelt. "It was Clark Upton who hired him." Sadness tinged her eyes. "Kindly, sweet Clark. He has a sister in St. Louis. She'll be devastated by the news."

"Where did Clark meet John?"

"We all met him for the first time at Fort Bridger. He was lounging around, not doing much of anything. I was told he had been hunting buffalo with a large party the week before." Diane paused. "Slaughtering them, would be more like it. Anyhow, some Indians, Sioux, I think, killed most of the hunters, and the rest fled to Bridger. Clark mentioned that John was thinking of becoming a scout, like his friend."

"What friend?"

"Groff. The man you tangled with at the sutler's."

A troubling thought inserted itself, and Fargo asked, "Whose idea was it to sign John on? Clark's?"

Diane's smooth brow furrowed. "No. Now that you mention it, I believe Bitterroot John came to us and volunteered his services. We had been getting by quite nicely on our own until that point. But with all the survey work we had to do, we figured it would be nice to have someone to take care of the menial chores."

"How long had you been at the post before he made his offer?"

"Oh, about two days. Maybe three." Diane looked at him. "Why? What are all these questions leading up to? What difference does it make which one of us hired him? Or when? He's of no consequence. A nondescript little man who will live out his petty little life in obscurity. Ignore him. I do."

From that point on, Fargo mused, he could no more afford to ignore Bitterroot John than he could a sidewinder in his bedroll. The man would bear watching every minute of the day, even after they reached Fort Bridger.

Diane departed. Fargo settled back again, but he should

have known better. This time it was Hester Williams who perched at his side, brushing her hair back from her shapely shoulder. Her throat, he noticed, was as flawless as marble.

"I wanted to apologize for slapping you. And for the comments I made. I was in the wrong, and I'm woman enough to admit it."

Fargo made light of it by remarking, "You're more woman than most, I'd say. You must have been the prettiest woman in your class."

For a professor, she blushed nicely. "As a matter of fact, I was the *only* girl in my class. Women in this country have a long way to go before they're on an even footing with men. Why, we don't even have the right to vote yet. We're treated as inferior citizens from the cradle to the grave. It's unjust, I tell you, and—"

Fargo had not meant to set her off again. Raising a finger to her cherry lips, he hushed her before she worked herself into a dither. "Save your breath for when you'll really need it." He casually ran his finger across her chin, then lowered his arm. The tip of her tongue flicked out, pink and inviting, and she promptly drew it back. "As far as having the right to vote, I wouldn't worry. Women will get that, and more, sooner or later."

"What makes you so sure?"

"Take a look at most any marriage. Nine times out of ten, it's the woman who rules the roost. The man will puff up his chest like a bantam rooster and act like he's the boss. But it's usually the woman who pulls the strings." Fargo stifled a yawn. The heat was getting to him. "Women always get what they want, given time. It's a fact of life."

"This from a man who told us he doubts he'll ever marry?" Hester joked. "Tell me. What qualifies you as an expert on the fairer sex?"

"If we ever get out of this fix we're in, look me up some night and I'll show you." Fargo said it half in jest. So he was mildly taken aback when her warm hand drifted to his wrist and her finger swirled in a playful circle over his skin.

"I might just take you up on that, handsome. I have a sneaking hunch Diane already has. And as intellectual rivals, I can't let her get one up on me. Can I?" Hester rose, winked, and was gone.

Fargo grinned. Of all the cockamamie excuses he had heard women use to justify going to bed with a man, intellectual rivalry had to be one of the silliest. Why couldn't she just come out and admit she was aroused by the idea of being with him? Just as the image of her stripped naked made his throat go dry.

Time dragged, weighted by millstones. When the sun reached its appointed position in the sky, one of the troopers bawled, "Here they come again. It's Red Band and a couple of his braves. Should we pick them off?"

"No firing," Lieutenant Jacobson commanded, bestowing a nasty look on Fargo. "Not unless I give the signal. And yell out if any other Indians show themselves."

"You're making a big mistake," Bitterroot John reiterated, but he did not interfere.

Hurrying to the bottom, Fargo exited the gully. The other two warriors held back as their leader brazenly approached. Red Band appeared to be unarmed but might have a knife strapped to his shin or his forearm. Fargo took no chances. Pointing the Henry, he said, "That's far enough."

The Ute tried to peer into the gully but couldn't from his vantage point. "Where be women? I pick one I like best."

"No woman, now or ever. Do yourself a favor. Take your warriors and go. From this point on there's no turning back."

Red Band grew somber. "I thought you different. I thought you smart. Now all soldiers die and woman still be mine. Maybe both women." Poking his heels into the bay, he trotted back and said something that sent the two warriors galloping off, one to the south, the other to the northeast. No doubt to relay Red Band's instructions.

Fargo rotated and took a single step. The buzz of an arrow in flight brought him around in a crouch, and it was well he had bent down. The shaft nearly took an ear off. He heard Bitterroot John yelp. Bringing up the Henry, he trained it on Red Band, who sat smirking at him like a cat toying with a mouse.

If the Ute thought Fargo wouldn't shoot, he was sadly mistaken. Fargo had palavered all he was going to. Red Band had refused to listen to reason, so what happened next was on Red Band's shoulders. But as Fargo bent his cheek to the stock, the Ute abruptly dipped down, sliding onto the off-side of the bay even as he wheeled the animal toward the cottonwoods to the north. All Fargo could see was a foot and a forearm.

It was a feat Indian boys learned almost as soon as they were old enough to ride. In the swirl of combat it came in handy. Warriors would swoop down on their enemies, unleash arrows, or hurl lances, then cling to the side of their war horses so they could not be hit as they retreated out of range.

But in this case Red Band miscalculated. It would have been impossible for a bowman to hit him. Nor could most white men have done it. But Fargo was widely considered one of the best marksmen on the frontier, respect he had earned by winning a number of highly publicized shooting matches against other competent shootists.

Centering the front sight on Red Band's forearm, Fargo lined up the rear sight with the front one, held his breath for a span of heartbeats, and stroked the trigger as delicately as if he were stroking Diane Marsten's marvelous womanhood. The Henry cracked, spewing smoke and hot lead.

Fifty yards out, Red Band's arm erupted in crimson spray. Gamely, the Ute sought to cling on but gravity defied him. He was spilled onto his side, then tumbled. The bay kept on going.

Fargo took a few steps to the right for a better shot. He sighted on Red Band's chest as the warrior heaved to his knees. Another moment, and the Ute's fanatical quest for a white woman would die with him. But as he applied his finger to the trigger, Red Band dived. The slug kicked up dust at the Ute's feet. Fargo worked the lever and swiveled to compensate as the warrior scrambled toward the riverbank.

It was then that the other Utes awoke to their leader's plight and came to his aid. Arrows whizzed from three or four points. So did bullets. Jacobson had been right about the Utes getting their hands on some rifles. Fargo had to skip backward as leaden hornets buzzed by and dirt sprayed upward on either side.

"Give him cover!" the lieutenant roared from close by. "Fire at the patches of smoke!"

The troopers opened up. Fargo snapped one last shot at Red Band just as the wily Ute slid over the lip of the bank and vanished. He could not say for sure whether he scored or not, but even from where he stood he could see a red smear on the grass. Another arrow flashed by, goading him into retreating. Firing on the fly, he skipped into the gully, nearly bumping into the officer. As soon as he was safe, the Indians stopped shooting. Jacobson bellowed for his men to do the same.

"Thanks for the help," Fargo said.

"I saw what you did." The lieutenant mustered a crooked grin. "And here I was having doubts about whether you were reliable. Damn near nailed the bastard, didn't you?"

Bitterroot John was coming toward them. "He hardly deserves a medal, Jacobson. Fargo should have done it sooner, when he had a clear shot. It was stupid to wait. It's stupid to sit here doing nothing. Give me that horse of his and I'll have more troops here in—"

Fargo spun and landed a right cross that smashed Bitterroot John onto his back. Straddling him, Fargo touched the Henry's muzzle to the man's nose. "One more word," he said. "Just one."

For tense seconds the gully was as still as a tomb. Then Private Jessup hollered. "Lieutenant! Mr. Fargo! Get up here, quick! Those Indians are up to something!"

# 8

Jessup was telling the truth. An awful lot of activity was taking place. Skye Fargo caught glimpses of Utes moving back and forth in the undergrowth along the Green River. For the warriors to show themselves, however briefly, was unusual enough. For them to do so repeatedly over the next several minutes was so out of character that Fargo began to suspect it was a ruse, that the Utes were doing it on purpose to attract attention. But why? The only reason he could think of was to draw all the soldiers to the north rim of the gully, maybe so an attack could be launched on the south side. But if that was their intent, they were in for a surprise. Lieutenant Jacobson had ordered the troopers on the south incline to stay where they were.

Then Fargo heard the faint drumming of hooves. Swiveling, he sought to pinpoint the direction. It came not from the north or south but from the *east*, from the narrow end of the gully where no troopers were posted. A concerted rush at that point would cost the Utes dearly, though, since the troopers could pick off anyone who tried to enter.

The hoofbeats drummed louder. Everyone else had heard them now, and turned. Fargo wondered if the Utes were going to ride right on down the slope. He brought up the Henry. The pounding was so loud, the Utes had to be close to the gully.

Then an extraordinary thing happened. Instead of a rider appearing, a large bundle of dry brush sailed up and over the gully wall. Flames and smoke spewed from it as it landed on the slope with a crackling thud, then rolled to the bottom. The next instant another bundle was thrown in, and another, both rolling further than the first one had. Smoke roiled along the bottom and up the two sides.

Fargo had to hand it to the Utes. Instead of trying to fight their way into the gully, they wanted to drive the soldiers out. Out into the open where the Utes could pick them off. "Throw dirt on those bundles!" he shouted. "Stamp out the flames!"

Jacobson mimicked the order. Half the men rushed to comply. Smoke had already filled about a third of the gully and was curling along its length in great gray coils, like a writhing nest of vaporous snakes.

Another bundle sailed into view. And another. The boys in blue were doing their utmost to snuff out the flames. One man tried to climb to the east rim to fire at the Utes, but the thick cloud drove him back, hacking and sputtering.

Suddenly Fargo heard new noises, a loud creaking and rattling, from the west. He investigated, sliding down to the bottom and hurrying to the gully mouth. Careful to keep his back to the incline and not to expose his whole body, he peeked out.

Four or five Utes had gripped the second wagon by the tongue and turned it so the rear end pointed at the gully. Now they were slowly pushing it toward the mouth. Evidently they intended to plug the opening, like a cork in a bottle, to keep the troopers trapped inside. Their strategy was brilliant. Once the gully filled with smoke, the soldiers would have no choice but to spill out over the sides. And Utes would be waiting to drop them in their tracks.

Fargo snapped a shot but the warriors ignored him. The wagon's bed protected them. Squatting, he peered underneath and saw a flurry of buckskin-clad legs and moccasins. The warriors were pushing hard to get their four-wheeled cork into position.

"No you don't," Fargo said aloud. Flattening, he sighted on the first pair of legs, on the foremost Ute's left shin. His shot elicited a yelp of anguish. The man toppled, clutching himself. Another warrior pulled the wounded Ute away from the tongue, and the wagon slowed. It was heavily laden, a challenge for the three Utes still pushing.

Fargo took aim again. The Henry boomed. He only grazed the ankle of another Ute, but it was enough to bring the man to his knees and the wagon to a lurching halt about ten yards out. The other Utes grabbed their stricken companion, hauling him backward, toward the river.

Fargo was pleased with himself. Red Band would be as mad as a wet hen. The plan had fizzled, costing two wounded men. It was doubtful the Utes would try something like that again. Rising, Fargo inserted a fresh round into the Henry's chamber and started to turn. He heard Jacobson bellow.

"Hold on there! What do you think you're doing? Climb down!" There was a loud thud. "Someone stop that man! But don't shoot! You might hit the horse!"

Fargo looked up just as the Ovaro bore down on him. Bitterroot John was in the saddle, slapping his legs and smacking the stallion's neck. Fargo tried to bring up the Henry but the pinto was on him before he could. He had to leap aside or be bowled over. A taunting cackle mocked him.

Releasing the Henry, Fargo lunged and wrapped both arms around the buffalo hunter's right leg. He clung on as the Ovaro swept out of the gully and veered to the south. The lower half of his body was being dragged, the friction and weight threatening to tear him off. He attempted to claw higher but Bitterroot John smashed a fist against his head, dazing him. It required all the concentration he could muster to hold on.

"Let go, damn it!" the horse thief raged, and hiked his Sharps to bring the stock crashing down.

Fargo was about to slip off. In desperation, he pushed his feet against the ground and hurled himself upward. His left hand closed on Bitterroot John's wide leather belt. He jerked his head back as the Sharps descended, absorbing the brunt of the blow on his chest. Simultaneously, he wrenched his whole body around, then heaved.

It was like flinging a sack of flour, only Bitterroot John was three times as heavy. Still, John was torn from the stirrups and toppled, cursing vehemently as they both smacked onto the hard earth. Fargo was on the bottom and had the worst of it. Hurting badly, he pushed the hunter from him and began to rise. He was much too slow.

"You son of a bitch!" Bitterroot John had lost the Sharps. Balling his fists, he clubbed Fargo's temples and face, so incensed that he did not think to draw his pistol or the big butcher knife strapped to his left hip.

Scrambling to the right, Fargo covered his head with an arm to ward off most of the punches. Twice he almost made it to his knees but each time he was battered down again. Marshaling his energy, he gave up trying to stand and instead flung himself at John's legs. It worked. Bitterroot John tottered to the rear a good six feet, giving Fargo the breather he needed to gain his feet.

"Damn your bones!"

Bitterroot John went for his gun. Fargo lowered his shoulder and charged, slamming into the smaller man just as John cleared leather. The Remington went sailing and the two of them tumbled. Both wound up on their knees facing one another. Hissing like a viper, the buffalo hunter resorted to his butcher knife. The blade was thick and wide and razor sharp. It shimmered as it flashed out and in.

Fargo had grabbed for the Arkansas toothpick but he had to hike his pant leg to reach it. Before he could find the hilt, the butcher knife streaked at his throat. Twisting, he gripped Bitterroot John's wrist. They grappled for control, John snarling like a rabid wolf. For a small man he was tough as nails. They struggled and struggled but neither could gain the upper hand. Finally Fargo let go and landed a lightning right cross that brought John crashing down.

Only for a moment, though. The buffalo hunter bounced onto his feet, and pounced, coming in low and fast, the butcher knife held close to his thigh. His beady eyes glittered with bloodlust.

Fargo barely yanked out the toothpick in time to ward off the first strike. Steel rang on steel. Undaunted, Bitterroot John feinted, then struck again at Fargo's ribs. A flick of the toothpick deflected it. Both of them crouched and circled, probing for weakness, for a fatal opening they could exploit. Fargo had a lot of experience at close-in fighting with a blade, but so did his adversary. They were evenly matched.

Weaving a glittering tapestry of lethal thrusts and counterthrusts, they fought in grim silence. Again and again Bitterroot John sought to penetrate Fargo's guard. For his part, Fargo employed every trick he knew, but one by one they were thwarted.

So intent were they on one another that neither paid any attention to where their struggle took them. Always striking and parrying, moving this way and that, forward and backward and from side to side, they strayed much too far from the gully. As became apparent when the gurgle of flowing water alerted them to the fact they were near the bank of the sluggish Green.

Bitterroot John drew back and glanced nervously around. He did not like being in the open. For that matter, neither did Fargo. Not with the Utes lurking nearby. The buffalo hunter redoubled his efforts, eager to finish Fargo off and get out of there. Their blades locked, separated, locked once more. Both of them strained to their utmost, pivoting for position, their legs braced like sturdy timbers.

It was Fargo who first realized they had strayed even closer to the river. His left foot slid out from under him, and when he straightened to gain solid purchase there was nothing under him to hold him up. They were at the lip of the bank. Off balance, he teetered.

Bitterroot John's chance had come. Smirking, he drew back the butcher knife for a final stab. At the same split second, a distinct *thunk* heralded the flight of an arrow. John arched his back, his mouth yawning in a soundless scream. He reached around behind him, lost his footing, and keeled down over the bank.

Fargo jumped down and crouched. None too soon. Another arrow whistled above him. Hunkering close to the dank earth, he slid the toothpick into its sheath, then palmed the Colt. The warrior who had unleashed both shafts was in a thicket north of his position. Fargo waited for the man to try again but nothing happened.

Twitching and gasping, Bitterroot John struggled feebly to sit up. He couldn't. His eyes darted to Fargo and he swore a mean streak, concluding with, "This is all your fault. You ruined everything. If you hadn't come along, the blonde would have been mine."

"Yours?" Fargo could not help asking.

"That's right. Groff had it all planned out. How I'd sign up to help those gals with their dumb survey. How Belcher and him would follow us on the sly. And when the time was ripe, we were gonna kill Upton and have the females to ourselves." A spasm silenced him momentarily.

"There aren't enough doves in Wyoming to suit you?" Fargo asked, not taking his eyes off the thicket.

"Plenty," Bitterroot John said. "But they're all as drab as burlap. They wear cheap perfume, and they treat a man as if he's a piece of meat." John quit twitching. His expression grew wistful. "Those Eastern gals, though. They're special. They smell real nice. And those bodies. Even with the britches and shirts they wear, you can tell they're beautiful."

"Worth being strung up over?"

Bitterroot John never hesitated. "Damn right," he barked, and paid for his outburst with another convulsion. Blood oozed from a corner of his mouth. "Those professors are the kind of females I've only heard about. Cultured ladies. Soft and sweet-tastin'." He coughed, then frowned. "We wanted to have us some real highfalutin ladies for once in our lives. You ruined the whole thing."

Had everyone in the territory gone women-hungry? Fargo idly reflected. He had yet to catch sight of the bowman. "Didn't you know they sent for me?"

"Not until a couple of days before you showed up. Groff was fit to be tied. He was countin' on being their guide. Belcher and him want you dead for spoilin' our fun."

"So I gathered." Pressing against the bank, Fargo raised up high enough to scan the area in front of the gully. No warriors were to be seen. The Ovaro was twenty yards south of the opening, standing quietly.

"We just wanted us some special women," Bitterroot John reiterated in a shallow voice. He was fading, his breathing labored.

Fargo felt no pity. The man had brought it on himself. The fate he had suffered was fitting, given that the buffalo hunter and the scouts would have murdered Diane and Hester to keep them from talking.

"Where'd you go?" Bitterroot John abruptly asked, glancing wildly around. "Why can't I see you anymore?" His eyes widened. "I can't see much of anything! It's all fadin'." Whining and blinking, he tried one last time to rise.

Branches moved in the thicket. Fargo guessed that the Ute was waiting for him to show himself. Smoke still rose from the far end of the gully, and he could hear Jacobson yelling about something or other. Tensing, he gripped the top of the bank.

"I hope Groff and Belcher get you," the buffalo hunter declared weakly. "Hope they cut out your guts and strangle you with 'em." Another brutal coughing fit resulted in John going limp. His eyelids quivered, his lips trembled. His last words were, "I just wanted a real woman for once. Was that askin' too damn much?"

Fargo vaulted over the bank and ran. Bent low, he zigzagged, reversing himself every few steps. He covered six or seven yards before the first arrow buzzed past. A few more steps, and another shaft narrowly missed him.

Few whites appreciated how skilled Indian archers were. Boys were given their first bows when they were six or seven, and practiced daily. By the time they were full-grown, they could bring a buffalo down with one or two well-placed shots. And they were incredibly quick. Some tribes held regular competitions, both for accuracy and speed. Fargo had been present in a Shoshone village when the men vied to see who could keep the most arrows in the air at once. The winner sent eleven skyward in slightly over a minute's time. Amazing by any standard.

Now Fargo was the target of a warrior who was almost as adept. Every few steps another shaft sliced the air. Every few steps he had to duck or dodge or spring to either side to save himself. Yet never once did the Ute expose himself.

Taking a few last long bounds, Fargo reached the Ovaro. He grasped the saddle horn and swung up. A jolt to his boot heel was proof of how close another arrow had come. Pricking his spurs sent the stallion galloping toward the gully. He was almost there when the warrior reared out of the growth to take deliberate aim. Fargo fired twice in swift succession and saw the Ute jerk, then drop.

Once under cover, Fargo reined up and hopped down to retrieve the Henry. Swirls of smoke eddied here and there, but most of the burning brush had been extinguished. Diane and Hester were closest to the west end, where the smoke was thinnest.

"There you are!" Diane exclaimed. "I was terribly worried. We didn't see where you got to."

"Where's Bitterroot John?" Hester inquired. "Did you kill him?"

"He won't butcher any more buffalo," Fargo said, "but I can't take the credit." Dropping onto a knee, he set to reloading both guns. The soldiers had spread out to await an attack that was unlikely to materialize. Red Band had learned a valuable lesson. The vengeful warrior would be content to wait until morning before trying anything else.

Fargo told as much to Lieutenant Jacobson a few minutes later when the officer asked his opinion on what the Utes would do next. "I'd have the men rest in shifts, two at a time," he recommended.

"We need water," the officer said, licking his parched lips. "That smoke made our throats raw. Mine is so sore I can hardly swallow."

Hester patted her disheveled hair. "What I wouldn't give for a nice long bath! When we return to the post, I'm going to have Major Canby fill a barrel with hot water so I can soak in it until I'm as shriveled as a prune."

The image she conjured tantalized Fargo. Seeing her ripe

figure bared would be a treat. So would having her wrap those willowy legs of hers around him. At the thought, he smiled. He was getting as bad as Groff and Red Band.

"Do you still intend to go after our mounts?" Jacobson asked.

Fargo nodded. Someone had to and he was best qualified. The green troopers would make too much noise. "Be ready to leave when I return. With any luck we'll catch the Utes napping." Literally.

"Take me along. You'll need help."

The lieutenant had a point. It would be considerably difficult for one person to bring that many horses back alone. But Fargo had no hankering to have to wet-nurse someone else, not when a single slip might cost their lives. "Your men need you here," he advised. "If I'm not back by three in the morning, sneak out and follow the river south."

The next couple of hours were deceptively peaceful. Fargo spent the time resting, his hat brim pulled low. He couldn't sleep, though. Several times he noticed Hester Williams studying him. Diane chatted with Jacobson. As for the soldiers, they were quiet for the most part, too overwrought to swap tall tales or jokes.

Rainbow colors splashed the western sky at sunset. Bright reds and yellows were mixed with bands of blazing orange, giving the illusion the sky was aflame. A subtle drop in temperature was a harbinger of a stiff northwesterly wind. Twilight descended, painting the world stark gray. But only when stars dappled the firmament did Fargo rouse himself.

Private Jessup was gnawing on his lower lip and glanced around, startled, as Fargo eased onto his stomach just below the rim. "Oh. It's you."

"The Utes would come from that direction," Fargo joked, pointing at the Green River, which was now shrouded in gloom.

"I know," Jessup said. "But my nerves are frazzled. I nearly squeezed off a shot earlier when the shadow of a bird passed over me."

"Try to relax."

"Impossible. I don't see how anyone could." Jessup pushed back his hat. "It's this awful waiting. Lying here minute after minute, hour after hour, waiting for those devils to do something. How does anyone handle this?"

"They get used to it," Fargo said. Most raw recruits were exactly like Jessup. The army trained them in how to load and fire a weapon, how to ride and march long distances, how to handle the worst of field conditions. But the one thing the army training couldn't duplicate, no matter how hard it tried, was the terrible stress of actual combat. *Being* in a battle was a lot different from *hearing* about a battle.

"I'll never get used to this," Jessup was saying. "Never knowing when an arrow might come out of nowhere. Or when a Ute might decide to sneak up on me and slit my throat." He shook his head. "No, sir. When my hitch is up, I'm heading home and going to work with my father in the bakery."

Fargo didn't blame him one bit.

"Do you—" Jessup began, and hesitated. "Do you think that means I'm a coward at heart?"

"Because you don't want your throat slit? No. I'd say it's more like common sense."

Jessup grinned. "Thanks."

The belt of vegetation fringing the Green lay serene under the stars. Not a hint of movement anywhere. Fargo hoped that most of the Utes had withdrawn to make camp for the night, leaving only a few to keep watch on the gully. If not, if all of them were still out there, reaching the horses would be a challenge.

Gravel crunched as Lieutenant Jacobson joined them. "You're getting set to go, I take it? Haven't changed your mind?"

Fargo did not respond. The officer already knew the answer.

"I still think it would be advisable to take one or two of the men along. We'll have enough left to adequately defend ourselves, if that's what you're worried about."

"I'm going alone," Fargo said for the last time. A check of the sky to the west showed several large clouds drifting toward them. Soon. Very soon.

More dirt rattled down the slope as Diane Marsten and Hester Williams came up. "Be careful, Skye," the blonde said. "I don't want anything to happen to you."

"Me neither," Hester declared. "We've hardly gotten to know each other yet."

Was it Fargo's imagination, or was there a hint of an invitation in her tone? "We'll have plenty of time later on," he predicted. Given he lived that long, of course. The clouds were almost where he wanted them to be. He quickly checked the Henry and the Colt.

"If I hear shots, I'll send men to help you," Lieutenant Jacobson offered.

"You'll do no such thing," Fargo told him, and nodded at the women. "Protecting them is more important than anything else. If I don't make it back, do as we talked about. Stick to open country where the Utes can't get close without being seen. Your rifles will give you an edge."

"Will do." The officer extended his hand.

Fargo appreciated their concern but he could do without the funeral atmosphere. "Keep your eyes skinned," he quoted an old mountain man saying, then slid over the brink before one of the ladies took the notion to give him a parting hug. Rising into a crouch, he angled toward a stand of cottonwoods.

He had picked the right moment. The clouds floating overhead had temporarily blotted out the starlight, casting the immediate area in somber darkness. But he had to reach the trees before the clouds went on by or the Utes might spot him.

"We'll be waiting!"

The cry came from Diane Marsten. Flabbergasted, Fargo glanced back and saw her head and shoulders silhouetted against the backdrop of sky. She was even waving. He couldn't believe it. He just couldn't believe that anyone could be so harebrained. Thankfully, Lieutenant Jacobson leaped up and pulled her down.

But the harm had been done. The outcry was bound to attract the Utes. They would wonder what was going on, and be on the alert. Fargo bent lower and increased his speed. He kept his thumb on the Henry's hammer, his finger on the trigger.

Two-thirds of the distance had been covered when he heard rustling in heavy brush off to the left.

Flattening, Fargo crawled the rest of the way. It was slow going since he had to stop every few feet to look and listen, but he made it before the clouds drifted eastward. Rising with his back to a bole, he froze on hearing a twig snap. Again, the sound was to his left. He did not move, did not blink. Elsewhere along the river crickets were chirping and frogs croaked in raucous chorus, but the wildlife in his vicinity was quiet. A sure sign the Utes were abroad.

A ghostly specter flitted into view, gliding from cover to cover in total silence. Fargo did not shoot or rely on the toothpick. He was certain the Ute did not know exactly where he was. So he let the man pass unmolested within twenty feet of where he hunkered.

Allowing a couple of minutes to elapse, Fargo veered toward the river. He threaded through the undergrowth as soundlessly as the warrior had done. Only once did some dry leaves crackle underfoot. Instantly, he dropped. But nothing happened. The strip of forest was undisturbed by hostile war whoops.

The sound of flowing water drew Fargo to the Green's bank. Paralleling the river, he padded to the northeast. He had a hunch the Utes had the horses hidden somewhere close to shore. As it turned out, he had gone slightly over half a mile when a pinpoint of light confirmed his guess.

It was a campfire. A small campfire, in a grassy oval hollow adjacent to the Green. On a makeshift spit hung the remains of a roasted rabbit. The horses were there, tethered in a string, as were some Ute mounts. Plus six of the warriors, including Red Band himself.

Concealed in a cleft twenty yards downriver, Fargo spied on them. They ringed the fire, seated cross-legged, speaking in low voices. Red Band bore a crude bandage on his wounded arm. Another man, one of those who had tried to wheel the wagon into the gully, had a splint on his right ankle and was using a busted tree limb to hobble around.

The rest of the band had to be watching the survey party,

Fargo reflected. Exactly how many there were, he couldn't rightly say. There had been fourteen originally, as he recollected. At least four were dead, maybe more.

Fargo was about to move closer when a stealthy tread warned him he was not alone. Spinning, he spotted a Ute coming toward him along the bank. The warrior held a rifle taken from a slain trooper and it was pointed right at him.

# 9

In the dark it was easy to misjudge. Skye Fargo was on the verge of firing when he realized the Ute was not taking aim at him. In fact, the man was not even aware of his presence. Eyes glued to the hollow, the warrior hurried by six feet from the cleft in the bank.

Red Band rose when the newcomer stepped into the circle of light. The man made his report, talking excitedly. Fargo knew a smattering of their tongue, enough to gather that it was the same warrior who had been hunting for him a while ago. At a command from Red Band, three others rose, collecting their weapons. They filed into the trees at a dogtrot, heading toward the gully.

Inwardly, Fargo smiled. Events had worked out nicely. Now only two Utes remained, and one of them was the man with the broken ankle. They helped themselves to what was left of the jackrabbit and settled back.

Fargo had a decision to make. Should he try for the horses now? Or wait for the pair to doze off? Waiting carried the risk of the others coming back before he made his move. Sliding from the cleft, he continued along the Green until he was above the camp. Then he sprinted into the woods and back-tracked, coming up on the hollow from the north instead of the south. From the opposite direction the Utes would expect.

It was a clever ruse, Fargo flattered himself. But as he came to the top of the rise in which the hollow lay, the wind unexpectedly shifted. Previously it had been blowing out of the northwest. Now it suddenly wafted from the northeast, against his back, bearing his scent toward the horses. Several lifted their heads and pricked their ears. One stamped a hoof. But none whinnied.

Fargo counted eight cavalry mounts, six team animals, and six Ute warhorses. More than enough. Snaking down the grassy slope toward the end of the string, he skirted a boulder. The Utes had their backs to him. One was chuckling. The other added a few pieces of wood to the dancing flames. Another ten feet and he would rise and rush them.

As if to foil him, the night was rent by gunfire from the vicinity of the gully. Both warriors rose, the one with the rifle cocking it as he moved to the other side of the fire. They listened as more shots rolled like muted thunder across the plain, followed by a series of strident shrieks.

Fargo grew worried. Had the Utes attacked the troopers? Or had one of the soldiers started firing at shadows, setting off a brief clash? As much as he would like to rush back and find out, he couldn't. Crawling closer, he stopped when a dun swung its head and snorted.

The Ute with the crutch glanced around. Seeing nothing out of the ordinary, he hobbled to his companion's side.

Fargo hiked his right leg to gain access to the Arkansas toothpick. He advanced slowly since he was at the edge of the circle of light. Five or six horses were watching him closely. At any moment one might give him away.

The Utes began to argue. As best Fargo could judge, the man with the rifle wanted to go investigate the gunfire but the man with the crutch thought he should stay. The prospect of counting coup won out. With a sharp gesture the first warrior jogged into the night. The wounded man scowled and muttered.

A golden opportunity had been dropped in Fargo's lap. He reached the string and slowly rose. The sorrel at the end eyed him warily, calming when he stroked its neck and whispered. A rawhide rope similar to those used by the Comanches had been tied to one of half a dozen saplings that dotted the hollow. It was the work of an instant to cut it.

Fargo roved on down the line, never doing anything that might spook the horses. The army mounts and the draft animals were accustomed to white men, and none acted up. But when he came near to the Utes' horses it was a different story. Several fidgeted, stomping hooves and tossing their manes. Fargo had foreseen they would. Indian mounts often grew skittish when they smelled the strange scent of white men, just as cavalry mounts did when they caught the scent of Indians.

Halting, Fargo let them become used to him. The wounded Ute had sat back down and was fiddling with the fire, poking a stick in and out. Fargo held out an arm for the first animal to sniff, then did the same for each and every one. They grew calmer, all except a big bay. It shied as he crept past, tugging at the tether.

Fargo moved faster. All it would take was one skittish animal to set off the rest. None of them had realized yet that one end of the rope had been slashed. They were lined up just as they had been. But that would all change if those near to the sapling took it into their heads to wander elsewhere.

Just a few more feet. That was all Fargo had to go. The bay nickered loudly, bumping into the horse beside it when it attempted to pull back. Naturally the warrior noted the commotion and reached for his crutch.

Fargo sank onto his left knee, wedging the toothpick under his belt. The only weapon the Ute had was a long knife in a beaded sheath. He would not slay the man if he could help it. A single butt stroke of the Henry should suffice. He peered under the horses, saw the warrior hobbling cautiously closer. The man spoke to the bay, which was prancing like a racehorse at the start of a race.

Circling around the last animal, Fargo was starting to rise when a figure materialized across the hollow. The warrior with the rifle had returned. Spying his friend, he hollered. The wounded man stopped. Fargo promptly scooted behind the string to avoid being seen. But now the bay and a cream-colored gelding next to it were behaving as if they were downwind of a cougar.

Of all the rotten luck. The second Ute hurried over. Fargo backpedaled and swung wide to the right. The warriors were looking high and low for whatever was to blame for their agitated animals, but as yet they had not looked in his direction. He dipped down into the knee-high grass to wait them out. Once the horses calmed, the men would go back to the fire and he could get on with it.

That was when the last horse at the other end of the string pulled loose. Seconds later so did another. They didn't go anywhere. Both were content to nibble at the grass. But the Ute with the hurt leg saw them and yelled.

Now the warriors would examine the rope, determine it was cut, and guess the truth. They would probably fire a shot to bring some of the others.

So much for the stealthy approach, Fargo mused, and broke into a run. He swept around the horses and was on the Ute with the rifle before the man could bring it to bear. The Henry crunched against teeth, jarring the warrior on his heels. A second blow, to the side of the head, split the Ute's ear and dropped him in his tracks.

The wounded man pivoted surprisingly quick for someone with a broken ankle. He swung his crutch as if it were a club, connecting with the Henry. Fargo sidestepped, whipped the barrel into the warrior's gut. When the Ute folded at the waist, Fargo snapped the stock overhead to finish him off. He was bunching his shoulders to smash it down when the crutch rammed into his groin.

Excruciating torment speared through him. His manhood felt as if it had been smashed to a pulp. Senses swimming, he staggered, unable to complete his swing. The Ute heaved upward. This time Fargo's elbow bore the brunt. The pain was beyond measure, rivaling the agony lower down. His left arm went totally numb, leaving the Henry to dangle from his right hand. Fargo retreated to buy breathing space but the warrior was a canny scrapper. The branch lanced at his throat, his eyes, his forehead.

Fargo evaded all but the last one. An explosion went off inside his skull. The night turned completely black and his limbs turned to mush. He felt himself hit the ground. His vision cleared just as the Ute towered over him, about to drive the branch into his neck. A forearm deflected it at the cost of some skin and a nasty welt.

Lashing out with a foot, Fargo slammed the man's good leg out from under him. Instead of falling to either side, though, the husky warrior fell straight down. The long knife gleamed dully as it greedily sought Fargo's heart. His hand closed on the other's wrist, sparing him from harm. But for how long? The warrior's face was a mask of hatred, his sinews corded knots. Wounded or no, the Ute was more than a match for anyone.

Fargo tried to push the man off but the warrior had hold of his shoulder. The tip of the blade was inches above his chest, poised to descend the moment he weakened. Stalemated, each exerted himself to the utmost. And ever so slowly the blade dipped closer and closer to Fargo's shirt.

The Ute's contorted face lit with triumph. Another inch and the cold steel would shear into flesh. He rose higher to add more leverage.

It gave Fargo a little more room to move, and move he did. Driving both knees upward, he succeeded in knocking the warrior off. Instantly, the Ute flicked the knife at his throat but Fargo was quicker. Rolling to the left, well out of reach, Fargo heaved onto his knees. His hand swooped to his Colt. As the warrior lunged, thrusting at his stomach, Fargo flashed the revolver into a short arc. The barrel caught the Ute on his forehead. Stunned, the man sagged but still tried to sink the blade in. Fargo had to pistol-whip him three more times before the Ute went completely limp.

Fargo felt like hell. His groin was aflame with pain, his left elbow protested every movement, and his head throbbed. He slowly rose, grimacing. Replacing the Colt, he claimed the Henry and shuffled toward the two loose horses. Neither gave him any trouble as he added one to the string and mounted the other, a sorrel. In less than two minutes he was set to leave.

He had done it. He had enough mounts for everyone. But he was not fooling himself. Trying to lead twenty horses linked by a thin rawhide rope in the dead of night through country crawling with hostiles would be a daunting chore.

Fargo had a plan, though. Rather than head due south, he rode to the Green, forded it, and looped to the southwest. He had to hold the horses to a snail's pace, with them bunched up tightly like they were. They made as much noise as was to be expected, enough that any sharp-eared Ute would hear them from a ways off. But it couldn't be helped. His thinking was that if he stayed well shy of the Green, Red Band's bunch wouldn't catch on until he made a beeline for the gully.

One of the horses at the back of the line began to give him trouble. The big bay kept fighting the rope, planting its hooves and refusing to budge. Twice he had to stop until the stubborn cuss took it into its head to cooperate.

The brisk night air did wonders for his head. It stopped throbbing, and soon his elbow felt better. But it was fully half an hour before his groin stopped spiking with pangs every so often.

Noting landmarks in the gloom was next to impossible. Fargo relied on his instincts to gauge where he was in relation to the gully. When he reckoned he was due west, he turned eastward, advancing more slowly than ever.

The most dangerous stretch lay ahead. He must ford back across the river and make a dash to the gully without taking an arrow or being shot. Or trampled, if the Utes caused the horses to panic.

Fargo cocked the Henry and tucked it under his right arm. Looping the lead rope around his saddle horn, he guided the animals to the riverbank. No outcries rent the dark. The Utes must all be to the north and south, he assumed, until he nudged the sorrel into the water and heard a warrior call out from the other side.

The horses splashed so loudly that Fargo could hear little else until he gained the opposite bank. As he climbed it, a figure appeared out of willows to his left. A shriek of recognition preceded the buzz of an arrow.

The moment of truth had come. Fargo banged off two swift shots, then gripped the rope and lashed the sorrel into a gallop. The horses followed suit. In a flurry of hammering hooves they raced in a compact knot for the gully's mouth. Suddenly

Fargo stiffened. He had miscalculated. Instead of being directly across from it, as he wanted, he had crossed about fifty yards to the north.

Fifty yards did not sound like much. But in near-total darkness, with nineteen thundering horses at his back and hostile Utes ready to separate him from his hair, fifty yards seemed more like five hundred. Fargo rode for dear life, constantly whipping the sorrel. He saw the undamaged wagon, then the top of the gully. It would not be long, he told himself. Before he knew it, he would be safe.

More shouts rose in fierce fury. From out of the trees to the north spilled Utes on foot and Utes on horseback. Five or six, all told, converging to head him off. A rifle boomed, the slug zinging high. Arrows came uncomfortably close.

Fargo bent low, gauging the distance he had to cover against how close the Utes were. He just might make it. Seconds later, however, a new threat arose, one he had not foreseen. The troopers on the gully rim opened up, no doubt with the intent of providing covering fire. But some shot too low, and now bullets whizzed past from both the front and the back. Any one of the slugs might have his name on it.

Fargo opened his mouth to bellow for the soldiers to cease firing, but didn't. They would never hear him above the uproar. He looked behind him, saw a strapping mounted warrior bearing down, and fired. At the retort, the warrior swayed and slowed. But there were others, yipping and whooping like a pack of demented wolves.

Fargo was almost to the wagon when the sorrel let out with a strident whinny. He did not understand why until her front legs started to buckle. She had been hit, and hit hard. Pushing off from the saddle, he flung himself as wide to the right as he could. It was either that or be trampled. His shoulder hit, searing with agony, and he rolled, throwing himself at the wagon and underneath the bed heartbeats before the space he had occupied was churned into fine powdery dust.

Confusion reigned. The horses came to a halt. Bunched together, they milled wildly, each seeking to go a different direction. From the north came the Utes, one warrior bounding in among the animals in an effort to gain control of them. Fargo took careful aim but the man was lost amid swirling horse-flesh.

Like the blare of a trumpet, from the gully mouth rang Lieutenant Jacobson's voice. "Charge! Charge! Fire at will, men! Stop them from taking those horses at all costs!"

Into the melee rushed the troopers, maintaining a skirmish line as they fired, reloaded, and fired again. At their center stood Jacobson, waving his saber and roaring like a lion at bay. The Utes retaliated in kind. In the inky murk, the jumbled press of animals and men was a scene of total bedlam.

At the heart of the firestorm, momentarily safe under the wagon, lay Skye Fargo. He saw a soldier go down, saw an Ute clutch himself and keel over. Some of the horses had broken free and were milling in fright, dashing every which way. A choking cloud of dust had arisen, blotting out men and animals alike.

Surging upright, Fargo moved around the wagon to the tongue. Several army mounts pranced close by, still connected to one another by the rope. Leaping, he grasped the bridle of the foremost, then hauled them toward the gully. What with the dust and the gunsmoke, he could not see his hand at arm's length, let alone the boys in blue or the warriors.

A two-legged shape suddenly barred his path. Fargo leveled the Henry but didn't shoot. He had to be sure it was a foe, not a friend. The dust parted, answering the question. "Jessup!"

The young private was coughing and wheezing and swatting at acrid wisps. "Mr. Fargo?" he said, blinking rapidly. "I can't hardly see a thing. My eyes are watering too much."

Fargo shoved the rope into Jessup's hand. "Take these into the gully and keep them there." Gripping the trooper's shoulders, he spun Jessup around. "Go."

"But the lieutenant and the others—"

"I'll help them," Fargo said, and gave the recruit a shove. Jessup stumbled, recovered, and hurried away, still coughing and flailing. Fargo gave each of the horses a swat on the rump to spur them along. Then, whirling, he plunged into the thick of the battle. A death scream sounded somewhere to his left. A gun discharged to his right. Horses appeared out of the haze, only to vanish again before he could reach them.

"Hold firm, men! Hold firm!"

The officer's command gave Fargo a clue where the soldiers were. He moved toward them, distinguished vague shapes, and hollered as a precaution. "Jacobson! It's Fargo! Hold your fire!" Another few yards and he came to their skirmish line now shrouded by the roiling veil of dust and smoke. The lieutenant was trying to staunch the flow of blood from a wounded trooper's shoulder.

"Fargo! Thank God! I came out to help but the damn horses are too skittish for us to catch." Jacobson's blue uniform was now gray, his hat had a bullet hole in it, and his cheek bled from a shallow furrow.

"Fall back," Fargo said. "You've done all you can."

Reluctantly the officer gave the order. Only three men were left to obey. Two prone forms sprawled in the dirt were beyond help. Fargo covered their retreat. Once they gained the gully, the cloud thinned. Diane and Hester were anxiously waiting, along with the two troopers who had been wounded in the initial fight. Jessup had brought the three horses and was leaning against the side, clearing his lungs.

The Utes stopped shooting and yipping. Fargo glimpsed riderless horses trotting southward, among them the big bay. It would be nice if some of the Utes were stranded afoot, he mused.

The dust took forever to settle. Along with the bodies of the two dead troopers, the ground was littered by two Utes and the sorrel. Another horse, an older one that had been part of the second wagon's team, was close to the river, standing still, a front leg crooked. Gleaming bone explained why.

Fargo probed the benighted vegetation. Red Band would lick his wounds and await daylight to renew the conflict. But the Ute was in for a surprise. Fargo did not intend to stick around that long. "We'll give the horses half an hour to rest, then head out."

Lieutenant Jacobson was swatting his hat against his uniform. He glanced up. "We can't. We don't have enough horses to go around. Only four, and there are ten of us."

"Eight will ride double, the other two will walk," Fargo said. "We'll take turns riding so it's fair. By morning we can be five or six miles from here." Possibly a lot more. It wasn't quite midnight, judging by the stars. By traveling without stopping they would gain a wide lead on the Utes.

Diane pointed at the trooper with the thigh wound. "He's in no shape to ride. It will start his leg bleeding again, and he's lost too much blood as it is."

"Would you rather wait around for the Utes to rush us?" Fargo countered. "I wouldn't." She offered no reply, so he went to the Ovaro, tightened the cinch, and slid the Henry into the saddle scabbard. As he forked leather, Hester Williams rested a hand on his leg.

"Where are you going?"

"The other horses can't have gotten far. I'll try to round up a few more."

Her fingers drifted higher, to his thigh, and she bestowed a smile on him that would melt a glacier. "I was so terribly wrong about you. I want you to know that, just in case." She puckered her full lips and whispered, "If we make it out of this nightmare alive, I intend to make it up to you."

"I'll take you up on that offer." Fargo reined the stallion around. At the opening he stopped just long enough to ascertain the coast was clear. A slap of his legs and he was off, cutting to the left to avoid crossing the open area. No shouts greeted his appearance. No Utes rushed from cover to stop him.

Forty yards to the south grew a strip of woodland. Fargo avoided it, preferring to parallel the river. In dank shadow he drew rein and rose in the stirrups to scour the landscape. The rest of the horses had scattered to the four winds. He trotted on, to the crest of a hummock that afforded a better view of the countryside. Not so much as a coyote stirred anywhere. The din of battle had driven the wildlife off, or into their dens and burrows.

Convinced he was wasting his time, Fargo bent the pinto's

steps northward. He was nearing the woodland when a large black mass moved from under a tree. Automatically, he flourished the Colt, only to discover a riderless horse. The rope was still wrapped around its neck, the other end entangled in dense brush. Thanks to the toothpick, in short order Fargo had the animal free.

Jacobson and Jessup were on guard at the mouth. "I didn't think you'd find one," the officer admitted. "One of theirs, isn't it?"

"Beggars can't be choosers," Fargo said. Now they had enough mounts for everyone to ride double. Their chances had improved considerably. Another couple of days and they would be safe and sound at Fort Bridger. "Double up," he said. "Time's wasting."

Hester Williams surprised him by offering her hand. "I'll ride with you, if you don't mind."

Diane acted flustered but she didn't object. Private Jessup had the honor of being chosen as her partner, and the boy actually blushed when she climbed on behind him.

Fargo assumed the lead. He tried not to think of Hester's arms wrapped low around his waist, or the feel of her bosom against his back. Or the stimulating scent of her hair when he swiveled his head to signal the others to head out. "At a walk!" he whispered. "Make as little noise as you can! If we're spotted, ride like hell and stay close to the river." He paused. "Any questions?"

No one spoke up. Clucking to the pinto, Fargo left the gully for the final time. Hester tensed, her arms tightening like iron bands. She had her cheek pressed to his shoulder, and now and again her warm breath fanned his neck and ear. It was difficult to concentrate but he managed.

The *clink* of hooves on rock and the *creak* of saddle leather were sounds they could not avoid making. A night bird hooted in the trees. A real night bird, not the bronzed buckskin-clad variety. For once things went their way and they reached the Green River without incident. Fargo rose high enough to verify everyone was accounted for. Jacobson and a trooper were next in line. Then came Jessup and Diane, followed by the other soldiers.

It was unnerving, that ride. The slightest sound had Fargo reaching for his Colt. He could not quite believe they were getting away with it, even after they had covered the better part of two miles. Hester Williams gradually relaxed. Whether by accident or on purpose, her hands slipped lower and lower until they practically brushed his groin with every stride the Ovaro took.

"Is it safe to talk yet?" she whispered in due course.

"What's on your mind?" Fargo idly asked. As near as he could tell, the Utes weren't shadowing them. But it wouldn't be wise for him to let down his guard, not even for a minute. He couldn't let her distract him. Then she posed a question that did just that.

"Do you find danger stimulating?"

Fargo wasn't sure he had heard correctly. What sort of idiot liked being shot at? "Did a ricochet hit you in the head?"

"No. Really. I'm serious." Hester shifted to make herself more comfortable. Inadvertently, her breasts wriggled enticingly. "I never gave it much thought before, but in a perverse manner danger can be quite arousing. For instance, when you snuck off earlier to find the horses, I couldn't help thinking how noble you are. It made me want to take you in my arms and smother you with kisses. What do you think of that?"

Fargo kept quiet. She really didn't want to know what he thought.

"We owe you our lives. You've gone out of your way to spare us from harm, for which I'm exceptionally grateful," Hester continued. "Maybe later on I can give you a demonstration."

"Later," Fargo agreed, wondering if he would be up to it. His groin still bothered him whenever he made a sudden move. As he did the very next second, when one of the soldiers let out with a wavering scream.

# 10

Skye Fargo wheeled the Ovaro and trotted back down the line. Everyone else had reined up and was looking to see who had screamed. It was one of the last two troopers. The man lay on his side in the grass, twitching and groaning. His partner vaulted off their mount, whipped out his side arm, and crouched.

"What's going on back there?" Lieutenant Jacobson bellowed. "What happened?"

An arrow that protruded from the center of the stricken soldier's back gave Fargo the answer. "Utes!" he hollered. "Get everyone under cover!" At any instant the warriors might unleash more shafts or cut loose with rifles.

Jacobson did not waste a moment. Yelling for his men to follow him at a gallop, he made for a stand of trees.

Fargo reached the last pair and quickly slid off. "We have to get your friend back on your horse." Bending, he slid his hands under the fallen trooper's shoulders. The other soldier complied without comment, equally aware of the urgency. Working together, they threw the hapless man over the back of the dun. "Now ride!"

The other trooper mounted and was off in a spray of dust. Fargo drew his Colt as he backed toward the pinto, scouring the night for the Utes. For once Hester Williams had done something smart and was bent low over the saddle. She straightened and helped boost him up by tugging on his arm and shoulder.

Fargo could not understand why more arrows had not been unleashed. Then he glimpsed a lone horseman burst from cover twenty-five yards away and race northward as if his mount's tail were on fire.

"There's only one!" Fargo declared, divining the truth. A single Ute had been trailing them for quite some time and decided to pick one of them off before hastening back to tell Red Band where they were. Fargo promptly gave chase. It was unlikely he could catch the warrior, what with the stallion burdened by double weight, but he had to try. Red Band must not learn they were no longer in the gully.

Professor Williams clung to him, gouging her arms so deep into his belly it felt as if she would squeeze him in half. Fargo raised the Colt but was thwarted when the Ute rounded a slight bend and cottonwoods hove up between them. He brought the stallion to a gallop, gambling everything on a short spurt of speed. It was the best the Ovaro would be able to do.

The warrior had increased his lead. He was now thirty yards off. Glancing over his shoulder, his features pale in the stark starlight, he grinned. He was confident he would elude them.

Fargo couldn't let that happen. By morning the entire band would be on their heels. It would be a running fight clear to Fort Bridger. Carefully extending his arm, he compensated for the range by slightly elevating the barrel, held his hand as steady as he could, and squeezed the trigger. It was a literal long shot. The distance, the darkness, the rolling motion of the pinto, all worked against him.

Yet the slug flew true. The Ute threw up his arms. Hurting, he clutched at his mount's mane and smacked his legs to prod it on.

Fargo didn't stop. Wounding the warrior was not enough. At all costs the man must not reach Red Band. He held the stallion to the same madcap pace, hoping against hope it wouldn't step into a rut or a hole. It was encouraging to see the Ute's animal slow a trifle, but not enough to enable him to catch up quickly.

For almost half a mile the chase continued. The pinto was showing signs of becoming winded. Fargo was afraid he would have to give up. Then the warrior's mount slowed even more and the warrior himself slumped over.

Fargo forced the Ovaro to hold to a gallop just a little bit longer. Gradually they drew close enough for Fargo to tell that the Ute's arms and legs dangled limply. Pulling alongside, he grabbed the rope reins and brought both horses to a stop. The warrior didn't stir. A check of the man's pulse confirmed he was dead. Fargo yanked the body off.

The extra mount was just what they needed. But Fargo did not hurry back to the troopers right away. The Ovaro needed a breather. He told Hester as much, finishing with, "Climb off. We'll walk a spell."

"Do you think it's safe?"

Yes, Fargo did. Had there been other Utes in the vicinity, the warriors would have shown themselves by then. Half in jest, he replied, "What do you care? I thought danger excited you."

"It does," she said, staring at the warrior.

Fargo swung Hester from the saddle and dropped lightly beside her. Holding onto the reins of both animals, he hiked southward. It would take an hour or so to rejoin Jacobson, but he would rather take his time and allow the Ovaro to recover than ride the stallion into the ground. He was not one of those who would kill a horse to save his own hide.

Hester was so close to him their arms brushed. "You didn't answer me," she said quietly. "Is it safe?"

"If it wasn't, do you think we would be doing this?"

The professor seemed to relax a little. Brushing at her hair, she regarded him a moment. "Always so sure of yourself, aren't you? Always so damn certain you know what's right?"

Where did she get that silly notion? Fargo wondered. It did not deserve a reply.

"I've never met a man quite like you," Hester went on. "There's an air about you. Something special." She gestured. "Even the soldiers are different. They don't radiate the same confidence you do. The same animal magnetism."

Animal magnetism? Fargo stifled a laugh.

"As for men back in the States, they're as different from you as night is from day. Most are so wrapped up in their work, they don't give thought to anything else. They eat too much, drink too much. They never get enough exercise. Did you know more men are dying of heart disease than ever before? It's their sedentary way of life I tell you. It saps their vitality."

Fargo was not interested in the least but he let her ramble on.

"Poor Upton was typical. Overweight. Lethargic. And he had little interest in women. A failing too many of his peers share. They would rather go to bed with a good book than a willing female."

At last Fargo saw where her rambling was leading. "Are you willing?" he bluntly asked.

"You'd have to try me to find out," Hester boldly responded.

They were close to the river, in an open area with an unobstructed view for hundreds of yards. No one could approach without being seen, not even Utes. A lone tree grew at the water's edge, an ancient lightning-scarred willow with drooping limbs. Fargo moved underneath and wrapped the reins around one.

"What are you doing?"

"Trying you," Fargo said, and suddenly whirled. She gasped as he gripped her by the arms and pushed her against the wide trunk, pinning her. They were nose to nose, mouth to mouth, her chest heaving, her eyes wide like those of a frightened doe.

"Here and now? The Indians might come along at any moment!"

Fargo noticed that she did not tell him to stop. "We'd see them." His left hand fell to her slim waist and she quivered as if cold. "Besides, my horse can use a short rest. Five minutes more or less won't matter."

A challenging look came into her eyes. Her ruby lips quirked upward. "Only five? Is that all you're good for?"

Her grin evaporated the next moment when Fargo plunged

his right hand between her thighs. His fingers were enveloped by warmth. He pushed them against her nether mound, pushed them hard, his knees pressing between her legs to part them further.

"Oh! No! What are you doing!" Hester exclaimed, squirming. "You can't be serious. Tell me you're not—" Her mouth went slack and she threw her head back. "Ahhhh. There. That spot."

Fargo was rubbing his hand back and forth. Her legs trembled violently and she melted against the willow, her own hands rising to his shoulders. Her breaths came in hot pants. She stiffened when he covered her taut breast with his fingers and squeezed.

"Uhhhhhhhh, I've never felt it so intense before," Hester husked. Her lips yawned wide, beckoning. Fargo sculpted his mouth to hers, his tongue delving deep. Her tongue rose to meet his, entwining in a sugary velvet dance.

Fargo had meant what he said about taking no more than five minutes. Checking right and left to insure they were alone, he undid her pants and pushed them down around her knees. Her underclothes were next. He roved his hand up and down and back and forth. Her inner thighs were silken to the touch. Her flat stomach was as smooth as marble.

"The things you do to me!" Hester said when they broke for air. "Keep massaging my breasts. Yes! Like that! Ah! Ah! I'm all wet down below! I can't stand it!"

Fargo wished to hell she would shut up and enjoy herself. But she was a natural born chatterbox. Everything he did sparked a comment. It was annoying at first, until he closed his ears to her prattle and concentrated on arousing her to a fever pitch.

"I love how your fingers feel! So strong! So hard! Oh, you're sliding one into me! And now you're touching me where—where—oh, my head is swimming! It's so delicious!" Smacking her lips loudly, Hester tossed her head from side to side. "Never stop. Never stop. I want more, more, more."

Fargo wanted to stuff a sock in her mouth but he had to settle for smothering her chatter with another kiss. She groaned and moaned the whole while, her hips grinding against his. When he inserted another finger and thrust it clear to the knuckle, she drew back and exhaled noisily.

"Yes! Goodness, yes! I can feel them! And something is happening!" Her eyelids fluttered and she rimmed her mouth with the tip of her tongue. "Plunge them in a few more times. I'm about to gush! I know it. I know, I know, I know— Ohhhhhh! I'm gushing, Skye! My spring is spurting!"

If Fargo had not had her nipple in his mouth, he would have cackled with mirth. No woman he'd ever known had come up with something like that. In devilish glee he drove his fingers into her "spring" again and again, while she smacked her bottom against him in perfect rhythm. For all her nonstop prattle, she was a hellion where passion was concerned.

Fargo lathered her other breast, then roamed his lips as low as he could go while standing. The dank aroma of her core wafted to his nostrils, stimulating him further. Cupping both damp mounds, he slid his other leg between hers and forced her thighs wider.

"I'm ready. I'm ready," Hester said. "Do me, big man! Do me as I've never been done before. Show me what you've got. Show me why Diane thinks so highly of you. Come on. Show me."

Fargo obliged by positioning his rigid pole at the entrance to her womanhood, then burying it in one smooth, powerful upward surge. He drove into her with so much force that he lifted her off her feet.

"Ahggggh! Yes! Oh, dear God in heaven! My head is in a whirl! I can't think straight!" Transformed into a wild woman, Hester kissed him, clawed him, braced her feet against the willow, and pushed against him.

Fargo should have been in ecstasy. But he had forgotten about his sore groin. Pain rippled through him. Not enough to spoil the moment, but enough to lessen his enjoyment. Gritting his teeth, he struggled to suppress it.

"I'm wet! I'm wet! Oh, I'm so wet!" Hester cooed. "You're so big, so hard. I can't stand it. I just can't stand it."

Fargo couldn't stand her ceaseless babble. Sliding his hands to her posterior, he gripped firmly and pumped his arms, adding momentum to her pelvic motions to heighten her thrill. She had already spent herself twice so he assumed it would be a while before she did so again. But he underestimated her carnal craving.

"I'm there! Feel it, Skye! Feel my juices rain down on your wonderful charger! The dam has broke! I'm flooding! Oh, how I'm flooding!"

It was the last straw. Fargo couldn't help himself. Even as he levered into her, he laughed. She finally clammed up and glued her hot lips to his neck, but he could not stop chuckling. She was too silly to be believed.

The Ovaro chose that moment to nicker softly. Fargo glanced around but saw no one. Still, it would be wise to move on soon. So, planting both legs, he pounded into Professor Williams with renewed vigor.

Hester started to shriek, then bit her lower lip. Tiny whines and gurgles issued from her throat as she slammed into him in a frenzy. Suddenly her whole body erupted in a spasm that had nothing to do with pain. "I'm coming! Coming, coming, coming, coming—" She went on saying it, saying it so many times he lost count, saying it as she thrashed like a madwoman, as she drained herself dry and coasted to a gradual stop.

It was then that Fargo's own release came. Surprise widened her eyes. She clung to him as if she were drowning and he were her sole hope of rescue. Repeatedly, he rammed his member home. He no longer cared about the discomfort. He no longer paid attention to the pain. His explosion was shattering, and at the pinnacle he reared up onto his toes, his hands splayed against the tree for extra support.

Exhausted, caked with perspiration, Fargo pulled out and leaned beside Hester. Her eyes were closed and she was smiling a secret little smile. "Enjoy yourself?" he teased.

"Ummmmm," she said dreamily. "You're everything Diane bragged you were. Now I can go back and tell her that you weren't only interested in her. She isn't one up on me, after all."

So that was what this was all about, Fargo reflected. As much as he would have liked to lie down and sleep until morning, he hitched up his pants and buckled his gunbelt. "We can't stay more than another minute or two," he advised.

"Too bad. I could go on for hours." Hester adjusted her clothes. Her fingers shook as she fastened her pants. "Look at me. I'm as weak as a kitten. No man has made me feel like this. What's your secret?"

"Clean living," Fargo jested. Overlooking his frequent binges on whiskey, cards, and women, it just might be true.

"If we get out of this alive, come visit me sometime. I'll show you around to all my friends. You'll be the talk of the town. A primitive among blue bloods, as it were. I think you'd enjoy yourself."

Fargo knew better. He had as much in common with highfalutin types as a bear did with a salamander. Give him the wild, untrammeled, open spaces any day over the cramped confines of city life. "First things first. Do you need help climbing on?"

"I can manage," Hester maintained, but her knees were so wobbly Fargo had to take her by the arms and steer her to the Ute's mount. It bobbed its head but did not misbehave when she straddled it. "Can you ride bareback?" Fargo had not thought to inquire.

"I can do anything a man can do."

That wasn't what Fargo had asked but he let it go and forked leather. The Ovaro was still tired but the short rest had helped some. He reined southward, holding the stallion to a brisk walk. The other horse fell into step without a lick of trouble. Hester kept grinning at him, and winking. She could be one aggravating female when she put her mind to it.

"Diane will never believe we did it," she said, accenting the *it*. "She'll think I'm lying. That it would be utter craziness, what with the savages after us. So I'm counting on you to verify my claim."

Fargo had no intention of doing any such thing. Bragging about sexual escapades was childish. But he humored her by smiling and nodding as if he agreed. Why set her off when they had so far to go?

"I intend to give Washington a piece of my mind when we get back," Hester mentioned. "Whoever planned our survey did not do an adequate job. We could all have been killed. I'm going to demand they send an entire company of troops out with us next time."

As Fargo recollected, she was the one who had squawked loudest against having Lieutenant Jacobson's men tag along. Now she wanted an entire company? "If you ask real nice, maybe they'll make it a whole battalion."

"You think?" Hester nodded. "That wouldn't be nearly enough, in my estimation. I'm beginning to see that those who want to place all the Indians on reservations might be right. I regret ever thinking differently."

Fargo had a regret of his own but he did not share it. She lapsed into silence, much to his relief, and they hurried on until they were within earshot of the spot where the warrior had put an arrow into the trooper. "Jacobson!" Fargo shouted, cupping a hand to his mouth. "It's only us! Don't let your men get itchy trigger fingers."

There was no answer.

"Strange," Hester said. "Are you sure this is where we left them?"

Fargo twirled the Colt out and advanced. Something was very wrong. He couldn't see Jacobson going off and leaving them. Except for the rustling of leaves by the stiff breeze, the trees were still. The stand was small, and in no time Fargo verified the soldiers were indeed gone.

"What could have happened?" Hester wondered. "Where's Diane?"

Fargo had no answer. There was a way to possibly solve the mystery, though. Leaving the growth, he ranged around it, checking every patch of bare earth he came to. It was too dark to tell much, but to the south of the trees and close to the water's edge he found where the soft earth had been freshly gouged by shod hooves. The officer and his men had gone on, then, at a brisk gait. He relayed the information to Professor Williams.

"It makes no sense. Why would they desert us? That lieutenant didn't strike me as the type to do such a thing."

They pushed on. The trail was easy enough to follow since the troopers never strayed from the river. Over an hour passed. Hester complained of being tired but she insisted they keep going. "I won't be able to rest until I know what has happened."

Another hour, and Fargo felt fatigue nipping at his mind. He had been on the go for far too long, with little food and barely any rest. His body craved sleep just as much as Williams did. But he shrugged it off. Soon afterward, a spot of sparkling light amid vegetation east of the Green alerted him to a campfire.

"Do you see what I see?" Hester blurted excitedly.

"Hush," Fargo cautioned. "Want them to hear you?"

"So? It's probably Diane and the soldiers."

"What if it's not?"

That quieted her. Fargo walked the Ovaro into a tract of widely spaced older cottonwoods. The campfire was bigger than it should be, certainly bigger than Indians would make. So the figures he saw sprawled out beside it had to be white men. Moving closer, he distinguished uniforms. A sentry stood slumped over a rifle, dozing on duty. Hester recognized them, too, and started to goad her mount on in her eagerness, but Fargo snagged her sleeve and whispered, "Do you want to get yourself shot? Do it right."

The sentry must have heard a noise because he stiffened and raised his rifle to his shoulder.

"Hail, the camp!" Fargo hollered. It had the effect of bringing all the troopers to their feet, some sleepily fumbling with their weapons.

"Fargo? That you?" the officer called out. "Come on in! It's safe."

Camp had been pitched in a small clearing. The horses were tied on the other side, most asleep, as weary as their riders.

Fargo drew rein and dismounted. "Took us some doing to catch up. Why didn't you wait?"

Jacobson holstered his revolver, his features growing deeply troubled. "It's Professor Marsten. She disappeared."

Hester was in the act of climbing down. "What?" she exclaimed. "How can that be? A person can't just vanish off the face of the earth. Speak sense."

The officer's jaw muscles tweaked. "There is no sense to it, ma'am. One moment she was there with us, the next she was gone."

Williams was so agitated she gripped the front of his dust-caked shirt. "Nonsense. There must be a logical explanation. If there is one thing my university education taught me, it's that there is a rational basis for everything that occurs. People disappearing is scientifically impossible. Conundrums like this—"

Fargo nipped her long-winded spiel in the bud by saying, "Tell us exactly what happened, Lieutenant."

Jacobson was mortified by his failure to safeguard Marsten, and it showed. "There's not much to tell," he responded. "We hid in those trees and settled down to wait. It was pitch dark. I refused to start a fire because there might be other Utes in the area." Pausing, he wrung his hands. "It was the damnedest thing, Fargo. The men were spreading around the perimeter, per standard procedure. Professor Marsten had gone to lie down next to a bush. I offered her my jacket to keep her warm but she declined, said I needed it just as much as—"

"That sounds like Diane," Hester interrupted. "She likes to pretend she's as hard as nails, but secretly she's a kitten. Why, I—"

"Let the man finish," Fargo said.

Jacobson's tone took on a note of acute dismay. "There's not much left. I saw her stretch out on her side. Saw it with my own eyes. Then I made my rounds of the men, making sure they were staying awake, talking to them to bolster their spirits. You know."

Fargo nodded. Although young, the lieutenant was a competent military man.

"Anyway, when I was done, I went back to the middle of

the stand and sat down to rest. I happened to look toward the bush, and Professor Marsten wasn't there." Jacobson glanced at his men, who were as upset as he was. "At first I didn't think much of it. I thought maybe she had gone off to heed nature's call."

Hester snorted. "Oh, really! Didn't you—"

Fargo hushed her with a jab of his finger. "Not one more peep out of you," he warned.

Indignant, Hester put her hands on her hips and angrily tapped her foot. But she kept quiet.

The officer coughed. "After a while I realized she was taking too long. I called her name but she didn't answer. Still, I wasn't overly worried. I was confident no one could have snuck into the stand without my men knowing it. And there had been no outcries, no commotion whatsoever."

"You conducted a search?"

"Of course. When it became apparent something was terribly wrong, I had every last man scour the trees and the area around them. We couldn't find a trace of her. Then Private Jessup gave us our first real clue."

Fargo faced the recruit, who shifted from one foot to the other. "What did you find?"

"It wasn't what I found. It's what I heard," Jessup said. "I was south of the stand when there was this low cry from even further south. I thought it was someone shouting for help, but it was smothered before I could be sure. Seconds later I heard horses running off."

Lieutenant Jacobson took up the narrative. "I ordered the men to mount up and we gave chase. But we rode for hours and never saw hide nor hair of anyone. Either Jessup's imagination was playing tricks on him, which I doubt, or Red Band finally got his hands on a white woman."

"Dear Lord!" Hester declared. "Poor Diane! In the clutches of those savages."

Fargo strode to the Ovaro and climbed into the saddle. "There's no telling when I'll be back so don't wait. Rest here until sunrise, then light a shuck for the fort."

"You're going after her now? By your lonesome?" Jacobson

shook his head. "Why not catch a few hours' sleep? Head out fresh in the morning, with all of us along?"

"Can't wait," Fargo said. He did not go into detail. Touching his hat brim to Hester, he goaded the tired stallion toward the Green River. He had an idea what had happened, and if he was right, Diane Marsten was in far greater danger than she would be in Red Band's hands. Truth was, she would be lucky to live out the day.

# 11

To the southeast loomed the jagged crest of a low ridge, and it was there Skye Fargo headed. The night was alive with sounds. Coyotes yipped constantly, occasionally drowned out by the lonely wails of wandering wolves. The cough of big cats and the rumbling grunt of roving grizzlies were added to the chorus at intervals.

Fargo wished he had taken a few moments to splash water on his face. Twice he had to stifle yawns. His senses were dulled by lack of rest, which could prove costly if he wasn't extremely careful.

But he could still think fairly clearly, and the more he thought about Diane Marsten's disappearance, the more positive he became Red Band had nothing to do with it. For one thing, there had not been any sign of the rest of the Utes during the long chase of the lone warrior. For another, the Utes would not have been content to snatch Marsten and be done with it. Too many warriors had been slain. They would want to take revenge on the troopers.

So if not the Utes, then who? Another roving war party? Unlikely, since few were abroad at night.

The list of suspects was a short one. Since Fargo had ruled out Indians, that left white men. Specifically, the two men who had intended all along to abuse the women, but whose scheme had been foiled by his arrival at Fort Bridger.

From the crest of the ridge a broad vista unfolded, an unending sea of darkness broken by patches of gray. To the northwest flickered the campfire around which Jacobson and his men were huddled. Much farther north another tiny speck of light hinted at the location of the Utes. Neither interested Fargo. He focused on a third ball of reddish orange, this one to the southeast. From ground level it had not been visible.

"Got you," Fargo said aloud.

He hurried now, since the pair responsible would not be content to wait until morning to satisfy their lustful urges. Two whole miles he traveled, through rugged terrain split by dry washes, outcroppings, and buttes. He did not spot the ball of light again, and he was about convinced he had overshot his mark when out of the corner of his left eye a faint glow registered.

Fargo heard voices long before he saw them. Leaving the stallion hitched to mesquite, he took the Henry and stealthily approached. They had pitched camp in a convenient coulee. Blankets had been spread out. On one lay Diane Marsten bound hand and foot and with a gag over her mouth. She glared defiantly at her captors, who were busy passing whiskey back and forth. Her hair was disheveled and her clothes were in disarray but she had not been harmed.

A log was added to the fire, causing it to fizzle and spark and expanding the ring of light. Fargo flung himself flat behind a bush as brittle laughter tinkled like broken glass.

"Told you it would be easy, pard," Groff boasted, and took another swig of coffin varnish. "Easy as takin' candy from a sprout."

Belcher had his turn at the bottle. "All I'm sayin' is that you take too damn many risks. There had to be an easier way of doing it than to sneak into those trees and carry her out like you done." He frowned in displeasure. "Hell. One of these days your antics will get us killed."

Groff was in fine spirits. Smirking, he gulped so greedily that whiskey spilled over his chin and down his neck. Then he belched. "But not tonight, pard." He winked at Diane Marsten. "Tonight we have us a grand old time. Before we're done, this city gal will be beggin' us to stop. We're goin' to do her like she's never been done before."

Belcher was not as happy. "We're steppin' over the line here, friend. If anyone ever finds out, they'll invite us to be the guests of honor at a necktie social. And I'm partial to breathin'."

"You worry too damn much," Groff groused.

"One of us has to."

Groff, incensed, shook the bottle in Belcher's bearded face. "What the hell is the matter with you lately? Gettin' soft on me?" When Belcher did not respond, Groff cursed, then said, "I swear! Haven't we gotten away with lots of shenanigans and never been caught? How about that time we jumped those Pawnee gals? You didn't object to pokin' either one of 'em."

"That was different. They were just Injuns." Belcher looked at Diane and his Adam's apple bobbed. "This here is a *white* woman. They'll track us to hell and back if need be to make us pay."

"Idiot!" Groff hissed, and smacked Belcher's shoulder. "They'd need proof we did it before they could lay a finger on us. And we have us an iron-clad alibi."

"Do we?"

"Hell, yes! That idiot, Captain Gleason, thinks we're scoutin' for Red Band twenty miles south of the post. He's the one who sent us, ain't he? He'll vouch for us when the patrol returns to the fort."

"Major Canby isn't a fool. He'll suspect we circled around to the north."

"So what?" Groff guzzled more whiskey, then stood. "Without proof, there ain't a damn thing anyone can do." Beady eyes twinkling, he ambled over to Diane and lecherously caressed her long hair. "Bet I shocked you something awful, didn't I, city gal? Comin' out of nowhere like I done and conkin' you on the head before you could cry out."

If looks could kill, Diane would have shriveled the scout where he stood.

Groff was full of himself. Tittering, he traced the outline of her smooth jaw with a grimy finger. She jerked her head away, and he laughed. His left hand pried at the knot at the nape of her neck. "Got something you want to say to me, woman?"

Diane had to spit the gag out to talk. She licked her lips,

then suddenly twisted and tried to kick Groff in the shins. He nimbly leaped aside, cackling with glee.

"Want to hurt me, do you? Want to maybe bash my brains out? Or gut me with a knife?" More amused than ever, Groff motioned at the encroaching night. "Tell you what. If it will make you feel any better, why don't you go ahead and scream. Get it out of your system. Not that anyone will hear you. We're miles from those soldier boys. There ain't another livin' soul within earshot. So be my guest."

"If I were a man—" Diane heatedly began.

"You'd what? Beat me to a pulp?" Groff snickered. "But you ain't a man. You're a woman. *All* woman, from what I can see. And it's about time I taught you how a woman should treat a man who thinks fondly of her."

"Lay a finger on me and I'll bite it off," Diane said.

Groff's brow puckered. "Yes, I do believe you would. You're nasty enough to do something like that. So how's about we do this the easy way?" Setting down the bottle, he beckoned Belcher. "Get over here. Hold her down."

Fargo rose and glided to the right, to a boulder wide enough and high enough to screen him. Resting the Henry across it, he pressed his cheek to the stock as Diane's wrists were seized and she was roughly shoved flat. "That's enough," he said coldly.

The two scouts whirled, and Belcher stabbed a hand at the Remington on his hip. Fargo stroked the trigger, the blast reverberating off down the coulee in both directions. He rushed his shot a bit. The slug cored Belcher's right shoulder instead of the heart, slamming the scout off his feet.

Groff began to go for his gun, too. But whiskey-soaked or no, he wasn't stupid. Changing his mind, he pumped his arms overhead, "No more shootin', mister. You've got us dead to rights. We won't give you a lick of trouble."

Fargo didn't believe that for a second. Neither was the type to give up without a fight. Swiveling the Henry from one to the other, he stepped into the open and slowly descended.

"Skye!" Diane said, tears welling up in her grateful eyes. She tried to rise onto her knees but couldn't.

"*Skye?*" Groff mimicked her. "Something tells me there's been some hanky-panky goin' on between the two of you." He sneered at Fargo. "Now I see why you were so all-fired set to be their guide. You miserable snake in the grass. You had the same notion we did."

"Not hardly," Fargo said. Belcher had sat up but was doubled over, blood seeping between fingers splayed over his wound.

"Shuck the hardware," Fargo directed. "Real slow."

They complied, but they were none too happy about it. Belcher, although in great pain and bleeding profusely, hesitated when his hand closed on the butt of the Remington. To prod him, Fargo swung the Henry's muzzle at his chest. "I'd think twice were I you," he recommended.

Muttering, Belcher flung the pistol over by Groff's. "So what now?" the latter asked. "You aimin' to turn us over to Major Canby?"

"Untie the lady," Fargo commanded. He shifted position so he could watch Groff closely as the scout knelt. Groff wore a crafty expression, as if he were hiding something. The man would make a lousy poker player.

"What about me, damn it?" Belcher said. "I'll die if I don't get to the sawbones at the fort pronto."

"You should have thought of that before you decided to go around raping women," Fargo responded.

Belcher was unrepentant. "How else do you figure we'd ever get to lay with a fine filly like her?" He openly leered at Professor Marsten. "Uppity types from the big city won't give men like Groff and me the time of day. They're too good for us, they reckon."

"And you've proven them right," Fargo commented.

Groff snickered. "Hell, Trailsman. You can't blame a man for havin' urges, can you? When you have an itch, you scratch it. When you're thirsty, you drink something. When you're hungry, you eat. Same thing."

"Is that so?" Fargo said. "Well, if what you say is true, then I should squeeze this trigger." Hiking the Henry, he sighted on Groff.

"Now hold on!" the scout bleated. "What in hell are you doing? I was talkin' about natural urges."

"And I have a natural urge to blow your brains out," Fargo declared. "Since you say there's nothing wrong with it, I should save the territory the expense of putting you on trial and just do it."

Groff tried to put on a brave front but he did not entirely succeed. "You're takin' what I said and twistin' it all around. Killin' is still killin', any way you look at it."

"So is rape." Fargo pivoted when Belcher turned toward the pistols. "A man never has the right to force himself on a woman. Any who do are scum."

"Like to judge others, I take it." Groff mocked him. "Never took you for a fire and brimstone sort." He was prying at the knots but not with much enthusiasm.

Fargo moved a couple of steps nearer. "Hurry it up. Red Band's bunch are in the area. They might have heard the shot." He was stretching the truth, since the Utes were too far off to have heard. It served its purpose, though. Groff worked faster.

"Red Band? So that's what happened to those missin' troopers. I wondered why there were so few with the lieutenant."

Belcher grit his teeth and wedged his thumb into the bullet hole. Groaning, he slumped, then remarked, "Wouldn't have thought that mangy redskin would be this far north by now. It was only two days ago that we struck the trail of a large band southeast of Fort Bridger. And we've been ridin' like hell ever since."

Fargo's interest perked. "You're sure they were Utes?"

"Hell, mister. You might not think much of us, but we can read sign as good as you can. Why do you think the army hired us?" Belcher grimaced. "It was a band of Utes, all right. Fifteen of 'em."

Fargo's brow creased. It could not possibly have been Red Band's bunch. That meant there were two bands of Utes roving that neck of the woods, and one band was somewhere between Lieutenant Jacobson and the post. It changed everything. Waiting until daylight to rejoin the troopers was out of the question.

Groff had finally finished untying Diane. She rose unsteadily, rubbing her ankles to restore the circulation. "I'm tingling all over," she mentioned.

"We're heading out as soon as you can sit a saddle," Fargo said.

Belcher looked up. "But what about me? I can't ride in the shape I'm in. You need to doctor me first."

"Take off your shirt," Fargo instructed him. After the scout obeyed, Fargo changed position so he could see Belcher's back. The slug had gone clean through, leaving a large exit wound. But it was the entry point that would not stop bleeding. "Lie on your shirt," he said. "On your back."

"Fixin' to bandage me? What are you going to use?" Belcher wanted to know as he slowly lowered himself. Weak from loss of blood, he closed his eyes. "I have an old blanket that would do if you cut it into strips."

"No time to bother with a bandage." Fargo had stepped to the fire. Selecting a suitable burning brand, he picked it up by the unlit end. Groff's eyes widened. Diane, puzzled, was silent.

"You'd better bandage me quick, before I pass out," Belcher said. "I can barely stay awake."

"This should help," Fargo said, moving to the scout's side. Without warning, he jabbed the tip of the flaming brand into the bullet hole. Flesh sizzled noisily, like venison roasting on a spit. The skin turned coal black. But the bleeding instantly stopped.

Belcher snapped up off the ground as if flung by a catapult, his mouth wide in a soundless scream. Features etched in disbelief, he gaped at the smoldering hole, then at Fargo. "You son of a bitch!" he said, and plopped over on his side, unconscious.

Diane, aghast, had averted her gaze. Now she stared at the charred skin, placing a hand over her stomach. "I feel queasy. Was that really necessary?"

"We can't coddle him." Shoving the Henry into her hands, Fargo said, "Cover them while I saddle their horses. If Groff so much as blinks crooked, shoot him."

The scout protested. "A person can't help but bat an eye now and then. Tell her you're joshin', mister."

Fargo did no such thing. It took the better part of fifteen minutes to get ready. He went to the trouble of rolling up the blankets and strapping the bedrolls on. Leaving anything behind was unwise. The Utes might find it. As he led the horses over, Belcher moaned and pushed up onto an elbow.

"I haven't hurt this bad since that time a mule stomped on me."

"Mount up," Fargo said, and to help the scout along, he slipped his hands under Belcher's arms from behind and hoisted him upright. Belcher feebly resisted, swearing lustily as Fargo steered him to the animals.

"I can't, I tell you! I'm not strong enough. I'll fall off."

"Not if your partner holds onto you," Fargo amended. "You're riding double." Virtually heaving the woozy scout up, he reclaimed the Henry. Diane mounted stiffly. A snail could have climbed on faster than Groff, but at length Fargo ushered them out of the coulee to where he had left the Ovaro.

The night had gone completely quiet. Whether from the shot or due to another reason was impossible to say. But Fargo didn't like it.

Belcher had not been exaggerating. He had a difficult time staying upright, even when he held onto Groff's shoulders. Fargo made them take the lead, the Ovaro right behind. Groff knew that trying to flee would have fatal consequences so he behaved himself.

It was slow going. Fargo halted frequently to listen. Along about four in the morning they came within sight of the cottonwoods. No campfire greeted them. Not so much as a wisp of smoke curled above the trees. Fargo hoped the troopers had simply let the fire burn out. But when he came to the clearing, the soldiers were gone. To say nothing of Hester Williams.

"Is this where you saw them last?" Diane anxiously inquired.

Fargo nodded.

"Where could they have gotten to?"

The same question bothered Fargo. He had advised Jacobson to light a shuck for the fort at first light. Maybe the lieutenant had done so early. Dawn was only an hour off, and Jacobson might have wanted to get the jump on Red Band. "We're heading for Bridger," he announced.

Belcher moaned. "Can't I rest just a little while? An hour at the most? Just until my head stops spinning?"

"No."

Groff was mad. "You can be a heartless bastard when you put your mind to it," he rasped.

"And even when I don't," Fargo shot back. They deserved no sympathy, not after what they had done. Shaking his head to dispel a few clinging cobwebs of growing fatigue, he spurred the scouts southward at gunpoint. Diane rode close to him, anxiety holding her own weariness at bay. She couldn't wait to catch up with Hester, and said so several times.

Dawn was spectacular but Fargo did not pay much attention. The chorus of warbling birds reminded him he hadn't slept in twenty-four hours. Most of that time he had been on the go. Small wonder he felt tired enough to spend a week in bed.

The rosy light of the new day confirmed Jacobson had pulled out early. Freshly churned earth testified to the brisk pace the officer held to. Fargo didn't blame him. Jacobson had Hester and the wounded troopers to think of.

The sad truth, though, was that it would take another twenty-four hours of solid riding, perhaps more, to reach the post. And it was unlikely the men or their horses could hold up that long. Out of sheer necessity, Jacobson needed to stop by sunset at the latest. So all Fargo had to do was stay awake until then and he could enjoy a night's rest knowing the women were well protected.

By the position of the sun it was around ten in the morning when Diane Marsten urgently asked, "What's that, Skye? Smoke?"

Fargo swiveled. Approximately half a mile behind rose a roiling cloud. "No, that's dust," he said. Dust raised by Red Band and company. The Ute had thrown stealth to the wind in order to overtake the soldiers before they reached Fort Bridger.

Groff clucked to his horse. "Let's get crackin', damn it. Those redskins ain't about to greet us with open arms. Red Band has a special interest in seein' Belcher and me dead."

"Why?" Fargo asked.

The scout would not reply.

"Don't tell me. You forced yourself on an Ute woman?" Fargo guessed. Groff's continued silence branded him guilty just as plainly as a frank admission would have done. "I wonder how many others you've had your way with over the years?"

Groff could not resist the urge to brag. "More than you would ever imagine, mister. When I want a gal, I take her. Whether she's partial to the notion or not."

Diane Marsten lit into him. "You're an animal, Mr. Groff. A ruthless, lecherous animal. You're everything I once accused Mr. Fargo of being, only you're a hundred times worse. No, a thousand. Creatures like you should be skinned alive and staked out on ant hills."

"Creatures like me," Groff said bitterly. "You heard her, Fargo. Proves I was right all along. Her kind look down their noses at anyone who doesn't wear fancy clothes or wash regular enough to suit 'em. Just 'cause a man has a little bear fat smeared in his hair don't mean he's an animal."

Diane fluttered her lips in exasperation. "You really don't understand, do you, Mr. Groff? You honestly don't realize how evil you are?"

"What's evil to you, lady, might be normal to me. Ever think of that?" The scout snickered. "I'll bet that's a scary notion."

"Shut up," Fargo said. He'd had enough of the man's prattle. For two cents he would save himself the headache of taking the pair back alive. "Just ride."

So ride they did, for another two hours, at a steady trot. The dust cloud dwindled but did not disappear, proving Red Band was bound and determined not to let the women slip away.

By midday the horses were tuckered out. Fargo deemed it

safe to rest for half an hour. On a grassy knob that jutted into the Green River they halted. While he kept an eye on Groff and Belcher, Diane watered the horses. He admonished her not to let them drink too much, as thirsty horses were inclined to do.

Belcher lay on his side, asleep. Groff glanced at the dust in the distance so often he had to rub his neck to relieve a crick. "How about a deal, Fargo?" he said when the half hour was almost up. "Three hundred dollars if you'll let us go."

"Not a chance."

"All right. Five hundred, then, in gold and silver coin. But that's as high as I can go. It's all the money I have in the world, all I've saved from my beaver trappin' and buffalo huntin' days. Got it squirreled away in a hiding place only I know about. What do you say?"

"Save your breath."

"*Five hundred*," Groff stressed. "That's more than most folks earn in a whole year. How can you pass it up? Think of all the doves you could bed. Or it could stake you to a week of poker in Denver or Kansas City. Most men would give their eye teeth to have that much."

Fargo was going to tell the scout where he could stick his money when gunfire erupted to the south. Rifles and pistols blasted in a rising crescendo, punctuated by whoops and screams. Not more than a mile off, he calculated. Lieutenant Jacobson had run into the second band of Utes. "Mount up."

Diane heeded him but Groff balked. "Give me a hand with Belcher," he said. "I can't lift him by my lonesome."

Fargo walked over. Groff smirked and started to bend, his right arm brushing his pant leg. He was still smirking when the Henry's stock smashed into his ribs, dumping him on his backside. More outraged than hurt, Groff flushed beet red and lunged upward. Or tried to. He stopped when he found himself staring down the rifle's barrel. "What was that about needing help?" Fargo asked.

"My mistake," the scout growled. "I'll try harder."

Belcher was ghostly pale. He woke up but he was as sluggish as a turtle, unable to raise his arms any higher than his waist. Of no help whatsoever to Groff, he sagged as limply as an empty sack while his partner grunted and huffed and puffed to lift him astride the sorrel.

Fargo assumed the lead. He could ill afford to have the scouts blunder onto the war party. First, though, he gave one of the revolvers he had confiscated to Diane. She accepted it much as someone might accept a black widow spider. Begrudgingly, doing so only because he needed her to help keep an eye on their prisoners.

The shooting soon ended, which did not bode well. Fargo tried to convince himself that Jacobson's men had driven the Utes off, that the soldiers were fine, but he was only fooling himself.

Rising in the stirrups every fifty feet or so, Fargo presently spied distant figures clustered an arrow's flight from the river. Promptly veering into the undergrowth, he was debating whether to go on by himself on foot when the figures filed northward. His worst fear became real.

They were Utes, nine of them, some wearing army shirts and jackets smeared by scarlet stains. Among them, riding double with a strapping warrior, was Hester Williams. The portrait of despair, her chin hung to her chest, her shoulders were bowed.

Diane went to lash her mount but Fargo snared her wrist. "Don't be a fool," he whispered. "You'd only join her."

"But we can't let her be taken."

"For the time being there's nothing we can do," Fargo said. "We'll save her, though. Don't fret." He wished that he felt half as confident as he tried to let on. Because once the newly arrived warriors linked up with Red Band's group, saving Professor Williams would take a minor miracle. He certainly couldn't expect any help from the troopers. Several vultures had already materialized and were circling on high.

# 12

Only after the Utes had blended into the haze did Skye Fargo urge the Ovaro out from under the trees. "Maybe you should stay here," he told Diane, but she insisted on tagging along.

Groff's cocky attitude was gone. He followed meekly at Fargo's bidding. As for Belcher, he was fully alert for the first time that morning and as nervous as a mouse in a barn full of cats. "We should forget about the soldier boys and save our own damn hides," he protested.

The troopers had been caught flat-footed. They had fought valiantly, taking the lives of six warriors. But in the end superior numbers had prevailed. Feathered shafts riddled some of the bodies, others had been gashed by war clubs or rent by knives. Lieutenant Jacobson had been one of the last to fall, taking two Utes with him. His shirt had been stripped off and his belt was gone but no one had mutilated him.

Fargo sat staring glumly down at the disjointed figure of Private Jessup. The boy from Ohio would never see his father again, never get to take over the family bakery, never know the simple joys of living a simple life. Jessup's thirst for excitement had been quenched, permanently.

"Shouldn't we bury them?" Diane asked. "It would be the decent thing to do."

"We don't have shovels and we don't have the time to spare," Fargo responded. He pointed at the six dead Utes, arranged in a row on a soft grassy mound. They had been cleaned of blood and gore and their arms were neatly folded across their chests. "The rest are coming back for these."

"How soon?"

"I give them an hour," Fargo predicted. Dismounting, he dashed from trooper to trooper, rummaging through pockets for personal effects he could turn over to Major Canby. The warriors had missed very little. In the lieutenant's pocket he found a letter from Jacobson's wife, declaring her undying love. In Jessup's, a pocket calendar with the days of the private's enlistment crossed off as he marked them down to his discharge date.

"What about Hester? I refuse to leave without her."

Fargo had a plan, an insane ruse that might work, but he didn't confide it in Diane. The scouts would overhear. "Light a shuck," he said, and galloped southward once again. Four or five times Diane called out to him but he ignored her. On a bank choked with weeds he eventually drew rein, declaring, "I'd say we've gone about half a mile. This should be far enough."

"For what?" Professor Marsten demanded.

"Let me have the pistol I gave you," Fargo said. Accepting the Remington, he slid it into his saddlebags with Groff's revolver. In exchange, he handed her Groff's rifle and a leather pouch containing ammunition. "Give me two hours. If I'm not back by then, head for the fort and don't stop until you reach it."

"I—" Diane started to object.

Fargo pressed a forefinger to her soft lips. She stared deep into his eyes and fell silent. "I mean it," he stated. "No one wants to die in vain. I'd like to know that even if everything goes wrong, you'll make it out alive."

"I give you my word."

Groff and Belcher were not particularly interested in the discussion. They figured that their part in the affair was done with, but they were wrong. Fargo drew his Colt, then indicated their back trail. "After you."

Belcher gaped blankly, but Groff was immediately suspicious. "What for? I'm not throwing my life away to save Williams. If she was stupid enough to be caught, she has to pay the price."

"I'm sorry," Fargo said with sugary sweetness. "Where did

you get the notion you could refuse?" Suddenly leaning toward them, he thumbed back the hammer. "I'd as soon shoot you now and be done with it. So which will it be?"

Groff's facial muscles twitched in raw fury. "I hate you, mister. I want you to know that. Just like I want you to know that one of these days I'll have the upper hand. When I do, you'll suffer as no one has ever suffered before."

"Save your threats," Fargo said, "and ride while you still can."

Wheeling the sorrel, the scouts retraced their route. Groff evidently assumed they were to go all the way back to the spot where the soldiers had died, but he was mistaken a second time. As he learned when Fargo hollered for him to stop. Mystified, Groff knit his thick brows when Fargo climbed down and directed them to do the same.

"What in tarnation are you up to?"

"Help your friend. And don't dawdle."

Belcher was strong enough to help out as Groff carefully slid him to the ground. They were in a weed-choked area flanked by trees. Large boulders dotted the open space. Fargo removed his rope from his saddle and tossed it at their feet. "Tie one end around your pard's ankles," he instructed Groff.

"Go to hell."

Fargo advanced, fully prepared to pistol-whip the scout within an inch of his life. But Groff's stubborn streak had its limit. Cussing luridly, the scout hunkered and bound his friend's ankles. Belcher did not resist.

"There." Groff growled. "Now what?"

Picking up the coils, Fargo circled the nearest boulder again and again, wrapping the excess rope around it, stopping only when there was just enough left to tie it off and reach Groff. "Lie on your stomach with your hands under your belly."

"God, I hate you."

"Just do it." Fargo squatted and wrapped the rope tightly three times around Groff's lower legs. Four knots insured Groff would not free himself any time soon. Verifying Belcher was securely trussed, Fargo rose. A bulge under Groff's pant leg reminded him of an oversight. Bending, he tugged the buckskin high enough to expose a dagger strapped to Groff's calf. "Almost forgot about this."

"You knew?"

Fargo tossed the dagger into the river, then strode to the sorrel, turned it to the south, and gave it a resounding smack on the rump. As the horse trotted off, Groff sat up.

"Why'd you do that? How are we supposed to make it to Fort Bridger without a mount? What in the name of all that's holy are you up to?"

"You'll guess soon enough," Fargo said. Next he holstered his Colt and rummaged in the saddlebags for their revolvers. Moving to a spot just out of the pair's reach, he removed the cartridges from both guns and jiggled them in his palm.

Groff was worried. Angrily poking Belcher, he snarled, "Help me out here. What is going on?" But Belcher only shrugged.

Fargo deposited the cartridges in a small pile. Beside them he placed the revolvers, butts pointed toward the two men. "If you lie flat and stretch, sooner or later you'll be able to grab them," he said. "Or you can try to untie the knots, but I doubt you can get them undone before company comes calling."

"Company?" Groff repeated. Blinking, he glanced to the north, then at the cartridges and the pistols, then to the north once more. Comprehension unleashed a torrent of profanity, ending with, "You miserable son of a bitch! I wouldn't do this to my worst enemy."

"It's more of a chance than you would have given Diane Marsten."

"What's happening?" Belcher asked, and was slapped by his irate companion.

Unfurling, Fargo stepped into the stirrups and reined on past the scouts. "Remember. Giving up won't do you any good."

"*NO!*" Groff wailed, lunging at the stallion. He missed. Rage and fear were mirrored by his countenance in equal degrees. "You can't do this! It ain't right! Take us back and we'll admit to everything!"

Fargo quickened the pinto's steps. He did not look back again. There was no need.

"For God's sake!" Groff screeched. "Don't leave us like this! We're white men, like you! And you know what they'll do!"

Fargo had to hurry. Every minute was crucial. For if the Utes were late, or he took longer than he anticipated, Groff would find a means of freeing himself and spoil everything. He sped along the trail until he reached a copse within a few hundred feet of where the bodies were. Leaving the stallion tied to a branch, he crept closer. A murmur of voices speaking the Ute tongue hinted that for once fickle fate had smiled on him.

Red Band was there, sure enough. So were fourteen other warriors, clustered around their slain friends. The dead troopers were being ignored, as was Professor Williams. She had been bound at the wrists but her legs were free. On her knees near the horses, she was stooped over in despair, her long hair hanging over her face.

Holding the Henry against his leg so the sun would not glint off the metal and give him away, Fargo glided forward. He looped to the right to come up on Hester, and the mounts, from behind. The wind favored him. And thick vegetation made the task of getting close an easy one.

Parting a bush, Fargo saw that Hester was quietly weeping. She was about a dozen feet away. The Utes were about forty, some even further. The horses had not been tethered but stood resting or nipping grass.

Fargo searched for a suitable small stone. Finding one, he waited until none of the Utes were gazing in his general direction. Then he threw it at Hester, missing by a few inches. She never noticed.

He tried once more, using a slightly bigger one. This time it struck her left thigh. She started, glancing up in alarm, perhaps thinking a Ute had hit her. When she realized that was not the case, she gazed around in confusion. Fargo was ready to wave an arm to attract her attention when she looked toward him—but she never did.

Hester slumped over again, a study in misery. She groaned loudly.

Groping the ground, Fargo came up with another stone. He cocked his arm, then froze. A swarthy Ute was ambling toward the horses. The warrior gave Hester a look of contempt. Selecting four animals, he led them toward the bodies.

The commotion sparked Hester to raise her head. "Please," she said to the warrior. "Do you speak English? Tell Red Band he must release me. I am an American citizen, and I refuse to be treated in this shabby manner."

Fargo could have told her she was wasting her breath. Even if the Ute understood, he would only laugh. And Red Band did not care if she were American, Canadian, or British. All that mattered was her being a white woman.

Patiently waiting until the Ute had rejoined those at the mound, Fargo focused on Hester's back and hurled the stone. It smacked between her shoulder blades. She jumped, and twisted so abruptly she nearly fell. Thankfully, none of the warriors happened to see.

As her eyes roved the brush, Fargo rose up high enough for her to spot him. To his dismay, she beamed, then opened her mouth to shout. Frantically, he motioned for her to keep silent. At the last instant she caught herself, nodded, and turned so she faced him.

It would have been better if she hadn't. Fargo ducked down. Red Band himself was staring at her. The tall Ute took a few steps but stopped when one of the warriors said something that drew Red Band to the bodies to examine one.

Fargo worried that Red Band might see fit to bind Hester's legs, or have her thrown belly-down over a horse. Or maybe put under guard. Snaking to the left so she could see him plainly, he beckoned.

Professor Williams hesitated. She shifted to see what the Utes were doing and saw several who had drifted to within twenty-five feet. Apparently she felt they were too close because she nodded at them and said softly, "Not yet."

But not softly enough. One of the warriors overheard and pivoted. His gaze followed hers. There was no time for Fargo to hide. The warrior's features rippled in surprise and he threw back his head to yip an alarm.

Fargo exploded from cover, firing on the fly while howling like a wolf. He winged the man who was about to yell, and dropped another who held a rifle. The blasts and his howls had the desired effect. The mounts broke and scattered to all points of the compass, some barreling right toward the Utes, who had to bound out of harm's way.

Hester was awkwardly attempting to stand. Fargo snagged her arm and propelled her into the woods. Backpedaling, he shot a man about to hurl a lance. Then he spun, seized Hester, and ran for all he was worth. Confusion ran rampant among the Utes. Some chased horses. Others milled about uncertainly. Red Band, however, kept his wits about him and bellowed to restore order.

Hester was gulping air like a fish out of water. "Must we go so fast?" she protested. "Couldn't you at least untie me? You have no idea of the ordeal I've been through! That heathen slapped me last night. Can you imagine the gall?"

"Save your breath for running," Fargo said. It would not take the Utes more than five minutes to catch their spooked animals, he estimated. Which did not allow for much of a head start. To gain precious extra seconds, he crashed through the brush like a bull gone amok, hauling Hester after him. She cried out when a limb gashed her cheek.

"Slow down, darn you! I almost lost an eye!"

"Would you rather Red Band got his hands on you again?"

That stilled her tongue. Fargo did not slacken their pace until they reached the Ovaro. Clamping his hands onto Hester's hips, he hoisted her up. She had to clutch at the saddle to keep from pitching over the other side.

"Wouldn't it be easier to untie me?"

Fargo could not spare the few moments it would take. Springing in front of her, he reined to the south and fled. The distant drum of hooves told him the Utes were in pursuit. Now it was a matter of staying ahead of them. Ordinarily, that would be no problem. But the stallion was as tuckered out as he was. It was tapping into its last reserve of stamina. A sustained chase would do it in, and spell their doom.

Hester leaned against Fargo's back for support. She was a

poor rider under the best of circumstances and these were hardly ideal. Bouncing and flouncing, she was nearly unhorsed when the pinto vaulted a log. "Untie me!" she pleaded.

Fargo covered the quarter of a mile to where he had tied the scouts in what seemed like mere moments. As a precaution he slowed just before he came within sight of them. It was a smart move. A pistol banged, lead sizzling past his head. Slanting into the woods, he circled around.

Groff and Belcher had gotten their hands on the revolvers and loaded them. Belcher was frantically working at the knots while his partner scoured the vegetation.

"I know you're in there, Fargo! Damn you!" Groff yelled. "Come free us and we won't shoot! Honest!"

Fargo did not stop.

Rumbling to the north snapped Groff's head up. "God Almighty!" he exclaimed in horror. "Hurry, Belcher! Hurry!"

"Why are they tied like that?" Hester asked in Fargo's ear. "Turn back so we can help them."

Fargo did the opposite. A prick of his spurs sent the pinto flying.

"What are you doing? We must cut those men loose. If we don't, the savages will be on them before they know it."

"That's the general idea."

"What?"

"We need to slow the Utes down long enough for us to get away."

"You can't be serious." Hester plucked at his shirt. "They'll be slaughtered! It's a breach of common humanity! I know they gave you trouble back at the fort, but that's hardly sufficient reason to make them suffer a fate worse than death."

"They were the ones who took Diane."

"It still doesn't merit—"

"They were going to rape her."

"Oh," Hester said. Then again, only louder. "Oh!" She coughed. "In that case, good riddance to bad rubbish. I hope the heathens chop off their manly members and stuff the parts down their miserable throats."

This from the woman who a second ago was upset about a

'breach of common humanity'? Grinning grimly, Fargo rode on. It was another minute before war whoops and gunshots mingled in a fiery din. The scouts held out longer than Fargo had reckoned they would, then the screams began.

Fargo counted on Diane Marsten being poised for flight and she did not disappoint him. The two ladies exchanged greetings as her mount fell into step alongside the pinto. For over an hour they stuck to a trot. When Fargo at last slowed, the stallion was lathered with sweat. It needed rest, needed rest badly. Angling to the water's edge, Fargo halted. "Ten minutes are all we can spare," he announced.

"My hands, if you don't mind," Hester said, wagging them as he lowered her. She showed more teeth than a kid eating hard candy when he obliged by slashing the rawhide with the Arkansas toothpick.

Diane was watering her animal. Downcast, she kicked a rock into the river and watched it sink. "Do you realize we're the only ones left?" she asked. "Poor Clark, that nice Lieutenant Jacobson, and all the young soldiers. They're dead on account of us."

"On account of that filthy butcher, Red Band, you mean," Hester amended.

They were both wrong, Fargo mused. Hatred was to blame, hatred and the raw distrust spawned by whites and Indians alike. So long as people like Hester branded all Indians heathens and warriors like Red Band thought the worst of all whites, the two sides would never live in peace. As more and more settlers flocked west of the Mississippi, more and more conflicts would result. And he would always be caught in the middle, part of both worlds and partial to neither over the other.

"I'm not going on any more survey expeditions," Diane was saying. "Let someone else deal with the danger and the bloodshed. I've had my fill."

"Not me," Hester said. "Think of the stories we'll get to tell at faculty meetings! We'll be the envy of everyone."

Fargo looked at her. The woman was an idiot. She shouldn't be allowed outdoors without a nursemaid.

"Why, I might even write a book about our adventures," Hester blathered on. "Publishers in New York would fight for the right to publish it. I can see it now." She gestured grandly. "*Savages and Sage* by Hester Jezebel Williams. It will sell more copies than *Ten Nights in a Barroom and What I Saw There* by that Arthur fellow. I'll be rich."

"Jezebel?" Diane said.

Fargo was tempted to remark that the name fit. But just then he gazed past Professor Williams, to the north, and felt his blood turn to ice. Astride four painted warhorses sat four sturdy warriors. Foremost was Red Band, whose hawkish face split in a smug smile. As soon as they saw Fargo notice them, they closed in at a slow walk. They were in no hurry. They had no need to be. Not when one of them had a rifle trained on Fargo's chest and another held an arrow notched to a sinew string.

"If you ask me—" Diane began. Then she saw the newcomers and recoiled, inadvertently stepping into the water.

"What's wrong?" Hester asked, rotating. Going rigid, she thrust both hands out. "No! Not again! I couldn't stand it!"

Fargo blamed himself. He had assumed all of the Utes would be delayed by the scouts. But Red Band had outsmarted him. The wily leader had come on ahead. Now Red Band had him dead to rights. He could resist, and die, or he could let himself be taken captive, and die. Damned if he did, damned if he didn't. In which case, he decided, the only recourse was to go down shooting and take as many of the Utes with him as he could.

Red Band must have sensed his thoughts. Pointing at the women, the Ute warned, "You try shoot us, we shoot them." At a sharp command, the warrior with the rifle shifted so the sights were fixed on Diane Marsten. The man with the bow aimed at Hester Williams.

Fargo had the Henry in his left hand, muzzle down. All he had to do was swing it up and fire, but he couldn't, not when the women would pay with their lives.

"What are you waiting for, Skye?" Hester chided. "*Do* something."

"He can't," Diane said. "Not unless we help." Her eyes met Fargo's. "No matter what happens, don't blame yourself." With that, she flung herself at Hester, tackling Williams and bearing her to the ground.

It caught Fargo by surprise. It also caught the Utes unaware. The man with the rifle was a few heartbeats slow in squeezing the trigger, and the slug intended for Diane's chest kicked up dirt instead. But the bowman fared better. His string *twanged*, the shaft streaked like lightning, and Hester Williams shrieked as the tip sheared into her calf.

Fargo took a bound to the left, leveling the Henry. His first shot smashed into the sternum of the warrior with the rifle. His second lifted the archer clear of the horse. His third missed, for as he worked the trigger Red Band plowed into him, the shoulder of the tall Ute's mount slamming him head over heels. He lost his grip on the Henry but he did not lose consciousness, and as he hit, he rolled and rose with the Colt sweeping up and out.

The other two warriors were bearing down on him, one armed with a knife, the other set to hurl a lance. Fargo fired from the hip, fanning the hammer, a trick only effective at short range. Two shots blasted as one. Both Utes tumbled, the man with the knife to rise again and charge, uttering a blood-curdling howl. Fargo fanned the Colt again, then a fourth time. The man would not go down. Fargo had to dodge a slash at his neck.

Snarling, the Ute coiled to strike. Astonishment riveted him in place. He touched one of the bullet holes in his chest, studied the blood on his fingertips, then pitched forward.

"Skye! Behind you!"

Diane's warning came too late. Fargo tried to turn but Red Band was on him before he could. He heard hooves hammer and a nicker, then a battering ram caught him in the side. The world turned upside down. Pain seared his shoulder and he was vaguely aware of rolling. The jolt of cool water on his face and a damp sensation from the shoulders down brought him erect in a rush.

Fargo was in the Green River, a foot from the bank. The

Colt was gone. The Henry was out of reach. To his left Diane and Hester were rising, Hester in torment, the arrow jutting from her leg. But they were alive, which was more than anyone might be able to say about Fargo in another few seconds. For out of nowhere Red Band was there. Fired by bloodlust, the Ute sought to ride him down, to trample him.

Fargo dived toward deeper water. He avoided the horse but he was not entirely successful in avoiding injury. A foreleg clipped him across the hips, and for a brief moment he feared his pelvis had been shattered. In excruciating agony, he rose unsteadily.

Red Band had wheeled his mount. "Now you die, white-eye," he said, and suiting action to words, he flicked his reins and produced a gleaming knife.

Three shots rang out. Three distinct shots, one after the other, and at each Red Band jerked as if pricked by an invisible spear. He wilted like a flower in a drought, slumping over as his horse came to a stop an arm's length away. Soldiers appeared, some seizing the lifeless Ute, others helping Fargo to reach the bank. Still others were tending Hester.

Amazement flooded through Fargo. Major Canby approached, his uniform caked with dust. Beyond were over forty mounted troopers. "How—?" Fargo said.

"You have Captain Gleason to thank. He came back to the fort to report that Groff and Belcher had deserted him. I put two and two together and came as quickly as I could." Canby gazed at the fallen warriors. "Not quickly enough, I fear. Where is Lieutenant Jacobson?"

Weariness caused Fargo to totter as if drunk. He heard Hester Williams answer. Then a soft arm slipped around him and warm breath fanned his ear.

"When we get back, I plan to crawl into bed and stay there for a month," Diane Marsten whispered. "Care to join me, handsome?"

"Only a month?" Skye Fargo said, and they both laughed.

**LOOKING FORWARD!**
**The following is the opening**
**section from the next novel in the exciting**
***Trailsman* series from Signet:**


**THE TRAILSMAN #200**
**SIXGUNS BY SEA**

---

*1860, where Kentucky and Virginia pressed against the*
*towering strength of the Appalachian range, when hate*
*and death cast their shadows over a growing nation,*
*from purple mountains majesty to shining seas . . .*

The big man's lake blue eyes narrowed as he peered at the
four horsemen who rode on the ridge just below him. He
moved the Ovaro slowly, held the horse almost at a walk as
the four riders moved back and forth, plainly searching the
dense foliage. The late-afternoon sun came in at a slant
through the red cedar and the shagbark hickory to paint the
ground with long streaks of gold that made the riders pass
from light into shadow. They moved forward in a straight line,
kept some dozen feet from one another, leaning from their sad-
dles as they used their rifles to poke and prod the dense brush.
They had no easy searching. Whether one trespassed through
the Alleghenies, the Blue Ridge Mountains, or the Shenandoah
Valley, the Appalachians hid everything in their thick, lush,
verdant cloak.

White ash, red cedar, sycamore, hawthorn and hemlock,
Joe-Pye weed, moth mullein, broomsedge and beggarweed,
blue grass, witchgrass and bristlegrass, the dark green, shiny,
thick leaves of rhododendron, the flame of azalea, the lemon
of the evening primrose and rose purple of bull thistle all grew

together, commingling, intertwining, creating a vast leafy carpet, side by side, around and atop one another, a profusion of greenery that was both welcoming and forbidding. Above it all, yet part of it, towered the mountains of the Appalachians. Skye Fargo touched the flank of the Ovaro with his left knee and sent the horse down an opening between ranks of red cedar that led to the ridge below and the four riders.

They looked at him as he pushed through the trees into the relative open of the ridge and reined up at once. "Where'd you come from, mister?" one of them asked, a burly man with a broad-cheekboned face and a bristly red mustache.

"On the ridge above you," Fargo said pleasantly. His eyes took in the four men in a single glance, saw hard-jawed, stern faces.

"You see a man running on foot?" the red-mustached one asked.

"No, but it's plain you're looking for somebody," Fargo said.

"Runaway prisoner," one of the others said, a thin-faced man with piercing eyes.

"You lawmen?" Fargo asked, keeping his tone bland.

"That's right," the man answered.

"Don't see any badges," Fargo remarked casually.

"Take our word for it," the man said, and moved his horse forward. "We've got a prisoner to find," he muttered, and the four men began their search once again, moving in unison. Fargo kept his horse in place. He watched the men ride on and call to each other. "Spread out more," the mustached one said. "Goddammit, where's the damn blood? There's got to be a blood trail. You know we got him. His saddle was covered with blood."

"I tell you he's lying dead someplace. We just can't see him in this goddamn place," another put in.

"We keep looking," the first one returned, and they went on out of sight into a thick part of the wooded ridge.

"Amateurs," Fargo hissed disdainfully. Automatically, his

eyes swept the thick, dense greenery. But it was no ordinary glance. These were the eyes that had learned to see as the hawk sees, to probe as the fox probes, to focus as the mountain lion focuses. These eyes could measure the way of a trail, a sign, a mark, a man, or a maid. These were the eyes of the Trailsman, and behind each lake blue orb lay the wisdom and the lore of the land and all its ways. With it came that special instinct born of the wild and touched by the wind, that sixth sense that went beyond all other senses.

The four men were no lawmen, no deputies. They hadn't the look of lawmen. They had the look of hunters tracking their prey. Skye Fargo grimaced. He'd come a long way to reach the mighty Appalachians. It had been a good while since he had ridden these almost impenetrable mountains, and he wasn't inclined to poke into things not of his concern. Besides, he had someplace to be and was barely on schedule. Nosing the Ovaro forward into the dense thicket of red cedar, he found himself thinking about the letter in his pocket.

It had summoned him, all the way from the great plains of the West. The money that had come with it was already safe in a bank in Minnesota. It was the kind of money no sane man would turn down, the letter no more cryptic than others he'd received in the past. Men who wanted a new trail broken had a tendency to be cryptic, he had learned over the years. Secrecy seemed a part of their thinking, as if a trail could be kept secret. He'd just finished breaking a new trail near the Overland route, and he'd left Kansas when the letter had arrived. He'd ridden the long miles leisurely and swung north only when he reached Kentucky, that land the Indian chief Dragging Canoe had aptly named the "dark and bloody ground." Riding over land that cradled the beginnings of America, he turned south when he reached Boone's trace, where less than a hundred years before, Daniel Boone had carved a path out of the wilderness.

It was this path that Boone took westward, across the Ohio and into Indiana and the untamed West beyond. Fargo had stayed south, took the Cumberland Gap, then rode north into the Appalachians as he decided to get in some early exploring of his own. He was still retracing his route in his mind when a sound cut into his thoughts. He halted, pushed aside a leafy branch, and saw a lone rider following the path the four men had taken. He frowned for a moment. This rider was a slender figure with dark blond hair cut short, a red-and-black-checkered shirt, and Levi's. But she searched the dense brush and scanned the trees just as the four men had done.

He watched as she leaned first right and then left out of the saddle as she slowly moved a dish-faced mare. She cupped a hand around her mouth to direct her calls in a hoarse whisper. "Kenny, it's me," she called. "Can you hear me? Are you there?" She paused, then moved on, peering into the denseness of brush, bushes, weeds, and trees, calling out again. Fargo moved out of the cedars, let her see him. She pulled up, alarm flooding her face at once. He saw her hand go to her belt, where she had a Starr double-action, six-shot Navy revolver.

He nodded calmly at her. "You looking for the same escaped prisoner those other fellers are looking for?" he asked.

"Is that who they said they're looking for?" she returned.

"Yep. You?" he asked again.

"I don't know," the young woman said, and Fargo's brows lifted, the answer not one he'd expected. She had dark blue eyes set in a face more pleasant than pretty yet with nice, full lips, a wide mouth, and a small nose.

"You don't know?" he echoed. "What's that mean?"

"I'm looking for my brother, Kenny," she said.

"What made you come here looking for him?"

"Been doing it for the last three days. Kenny usually visits at this time of the month. I rode up, saw those four, and got really frightened. I heard them say they'd shot somebody," the young woman said.

"What makes you think it was your brother they shot?" Fargo asked.

"Damn few folks would be coming up here. I knew Kenny

was due. Maybe they're dry-gulchers that jumped him," she said.

Fargo's lips pursed. "Not likely," he murmured.

"Why not?" She frowned.

"Dry-gulchers look for a quick hit usually. That means they go where they have opportunities, outside a town, a stage route, places well traveled. They wouldn't come looking for a victim in these godforsaken mountains," Fargo said.

"They shot somebody. They're trying to find a blood trail," she said.

"I know. I heard," he said.

"It could have been Kenny," she insisted. "I want to be sure. I'm going to keep looking, for whoever it is."

"And making the same mistakes they are," he said.

"How?" She frowned.

"You're looking for blood on the tops of leaves and bushes, just as they are."

"That's where it'd be," she said.

"If he's running," Fargo said. "That's when a wounded man will drop blood on the tops of leaves and bushes. If he's crawling, he'll leave a blood trail on the underside of leaves and along stems."

"You think he's crawling?" she asked, her blue eyes wide.

"I'd bet on it," Fargo said.

"How do you know so much?" the young woman asked.

"Name's Fargo, Skye Fargo. Some call me the Trailsman," he said.

"Linda Corrigan," she said. "Help me look. Please. It could be my brother. Maybe he got into a fight with them."

Fargo let a sigh escape his lips as he swung from the saddle and started to walk across the ground at right angles to where the four men had searched. As he went into a crouch and began to part brush, leaves, and bushes, he saw her slide from her horse and begin to search as he did. But Fargo didn't search for blood at first. Suddenly he found what he sought, stems and leaves that were bruised near their base. The spots of blood came quickly after that. "Over here," he called as he pushed on, staying in a crouch. Linda Corrigan was hurrying toward him when he saw the figure lying facedown in thick shrubbery. He knelt beside it, turned the figure on its back and saw a young man half conscious with the same dark blond hair that Linda Corrigan had. The man was bleeding heavily from a hole through his throat.

"Oh, God. Oh, God. It's Kenny," Linda said as she reached him, dropping to one knee beside him.

"He's still alive, but that's a nasty wound," Fargo said.

"We have to stop the bleeding," she said, her hands tearing at the red-and-black-checkered shirt. She pulled it off, and Fargo saw she wore a slip underneath that clung to small, up-turned breasts that pressed into the thin fabric. He helped her wrap the shirtsleeves around the young man's neck.

"I'll finish. Get your horse," he said.

"I've a cabin. Help me get him there," she said, and Fargo finished wrapping the makeshift bandage as she rose and ran back to the gray mare. She returned in moments, and Fargo carefully lifted the limp figure onto her horse and placed him on his stomach as Linda swung onto the saddle behind him.

"Slowly, real slowly," Fargo said as he went back to the Ovaro and rode behind her as she climbed a narrow trail up to the ridge above. Once on the ridge, she turned west, and he rode beside her. She had a firm, lean figure, nice strong shoulders, and the smallish breasts hardly moved as she rode, everything about her tight and lean.

"Bastards," she murmured through tight lips. "Whoever they are." He didn't answer and turned the question in his mind. No dry-gulchers, he reiterated silently. And no chance meeting that had resulted in an argument. They'd have left him for dead and gone their way. But these men searched after him, were still searching, purposeful, determined to finish him. They had reasons, and Fargo glanced at Linda Corrigan and wondered how much she knew about her brother. She rode with her jaw set, and in her dark blue eyes he saw pain and anger.

"You know any reasons why they'd want to shoot your brother?" he asked.

"He was into something. He wouldn't tell me what," Linda Corrigan said. "Maybe he will now."

"You were very close?" Fargo asked.

"When he was growing up, he was a great kid brother," she said, then fell silent with her own thoughts. He wondered what she was doing up here in the wildness of the Blue Ridge Mountains. The sun still found its way through the towering sycamores, bitternut, and black oak, and Fargo saw a road suddenly appear and curve around a high hill. He rounded the curve with Linda, and the cabin appeared. Only it was more of a long log house than a cabin, with a smaller structure alongside it.

Fronting the house a long stretch of canvas attached to tall poles afforded a cover that plainly could be rolled partly or completely back. Beneath the canvas roof were rows of clay pots and long wooden boxes, all with plants growing in them. A workbench to one side was covered with glass vials containing seeds. He was staring at everything as Linda drew up in front of the house, where the door hung open. Dismounting, Fargo lifted the unconscious form from the horse and followed Linda into the house, saw a large room comfortably furnished with a sofa, chairs, and dining table. A cot rested against one wall, and he lowered Kenny Corrigan onto it. Linda immediately loosened the makeshift bandage around her brother's neck. Blood began flowing from the wound at once, and Linda disappeared, returned with a proper bandage, and wrapped it around the man's neck. She turned to Fargo and met his eyes. "It won't do, will it?" she said.

"No. He needs a doc and fast," Fargo said.

"We'll take him to Pine Hollow. It's at the foot of the mountain," Linda said.

"There's a doc up here in these mountains?" Fargo frowned.

"Doc Benson," she said. "There are mountain people up here, families, that need tending to. Then there are trappers, hunters, and woodsmen who get themselves hurt in one way or another. He's no fancy hospital doctor, but he manages. Real serious cases he can't handle he sends down to Virginia, if they can make it. There's a hospital at Roanoke. I'll use my wagon. Kenny won't make it by horse." She went off, returned in a moment with a green shirt on, and he followed her outside to the rear of the house, where he saw an Owensboro huckster wagon with flare board sides and a drop end gate.

He helped her hitch the gray mare to the wagon. "There's only one road down," she said as he carried the unconscious form from the house and laid it on a blanket she had spread in the wagon. She climbed onto the seat and took the reins.

"Want me to come along?" he asked.

Her hand touched his arm, stayed there. "I'd like that," she said, her blue eyes grave. "If it weren't for you, he might still be back there dead. You can leave your horse. He'll find the oat bin around back."

"You can be sure of that," Fargo said and pulled himself onto the seat beside her. He glanced again at the canvas-roofed area, the rows of clay pots, as she drove past. "What is all this?" he asked. "And what are you doing up here in the middle of the Appalachians? You're no mountain girl."

"I sometimes think I'm becoming one," she said. "I'm a botanist. I'm making a listing and a study of every variety of plant, flower, shrub, seed, and tree in the mountains, starting here in the Blue Ridge. The state of Virginia gave me a grant to do it. It'll be the only study of its kind. It'll take years to finish, of course."

"Then you don't spend all your time up here in the mountains."

"I try to get away every month or two for a few days," she said.

"Where?"

"A family house in Virginia, north of Shenandoah. It lets

164

me visit Fredericksburg or Alexandria," Linda said. "Lets me visit the social scene."

"You're an unusual combination of things, I'd say," Fargo remarked.

"I get caught up in whatever I do, my work or whatever is important to me," Linda said. "Why are you here, Fargo?"

"I'm on my way to see a man who wants me to break a new trail through the Appalachians," he told her.

She let her dark blue eyes study him for a long, thoughtful moment. "I imagine you'll do it," she said. "And I'll be sort of sorry."

"Sorry?" He frowned.

"I like the Appalachians the way they are, majestic, unspoiled, uncontaminated, no man-made trails, no incursions by hordes of people."

"Or cattle," he said.

"Or cattle," she agreed.

"You may have it your way," he said, his eyes going to the towering green peaks. "These are formidable mountains. They're beautiful and forbidding." His words ended as dusk began to lower, enshrouding the tall peaks. The road turned and twisted, but Linda drove well, handled the wagon with ease. An unusual and complicated young woman, he decided, with her own, understated attractiveness. Night had descended over the Appalachians when they reached Pine Hollow, a cleared circle of land at the foot of three mountains and surrounded by Virginia pine, fragrant with their short needles and prickly cones. Doc Benson's quarters consisted of two almost identical houses that turned out to be primitively equipped, yet neat and clean.

Doc Benson greeted them as they drove up, a tall, spare man with a face both ascetic and strong. A woman with her hair pulled back and wearing a white apron stood by. The doctor looked at Kenny Corrigan and helped Fargo move him inside to a clean bed, where he examined the young man more carefully. "He's lost a lot of blood, too much," the doctor told

Linda. "I'll try to bring him around. Meanwhile, I'll put a tube into that hole in his throat to stop him from losing more blood and dissipating air. I think you should come back in the morning."

"You don't sound hopeful," Linda said.

"I'm not," Doc Benson said honestly. "If we can get him stabilized, we can try getting him to Roanoke."

"I'll be back in the morning," Linda said. "Do your best. But I know you'll do that," she added. She took hold of Fargo's arm as she walked into the night, paused at the carriage.

"Want me to drive?" he asked, and she nodded.

"Just follow the road," she said, and he took the reins. She sat close beside him, and the moon came up to light the road as it curved and twisted upward. She rode in silence until they returned to her place, where she hurried inside first and lighted two kerosene lamps. "The cabin alongside the house is for guests. I'd like you to stay the night. I owe you. Kenny owes you," she said. "There's a covered stable in the back. That's a fine Ovaro, too fine to leave out all night."

"I'll stay. I'm feeling the ride over here," Fargo said. She handed him one of the lamps, and he took it, then went outside, unsaddled, and stabled the pinto in a small, three-horse structure that was sturdier than it appeared at first sight. He went to the smaller cabin at the end of the house and found it clean, a dresser and good-sized bed against one wall, a reed rug on the floor. He began to undress and was down to his trousers when he heard footsteps at the door. Linda came in carrying a small tray with sandwiches and a coffee mug.

"Thought you could use something to eat," she said, and set the tray down on a small end table. She wore a knee-length blue nightdress that made her look almost little girllike as it clung to her small breasts and lay against her slender body.

"Thanks," he said, and saw her eyes travel slowly across the muscled beauty of his torso. As she lowered herself to the edge of the bed, he felt her eyes staying on him. "I feel as though I'm one of the seeds you study." He smiled.

"Sorry." She laughed softly. "I was just wondering if all trailsmen are as uncommonly handsome as you."

"You've been alone in these mountains too long," he said.

"Probably," she agreed. "Maybe it's made me restless but not blind."

"One thing affects another," he laughed between bites of the sandwich.

"Not with me. I'm a scientist. I know about keeping things separate," she said.

"I imagine you do," he said honestly. "You keep your own contrasts separated, too, I'll wager."

"What contrasts?" she questioned.

"The botanist, the young woman scientist, the dedicated professional, and the little-girl lookalike in that nightdress," he said.

A slow smile spread across her wide mouth, reluctant admiration curled inside it. "You're very astute," she murmured.

"I read signs, remember?" he said, finishing the meal.

She rose, came to stand before him, and placed both hands on the muscled smoothness of his chest. Her lips lifted and came to his, lingered, soft and warm, and her breath came in short gasps until finally she pulled away, her fingers curling against his naked torso. "How do you read that?" she asked softly. "Scientist or little girl?"

"Maybe some of both," he said.

"You're wrong about both. It was a simple thank-you for helping me," she said.

He smiled. "Bullshit, honey," he said. She gave a little shrug with her half smile, turned away and glided from the cabin.

"Good night, Fargo," she called back. He laughed as he finished undressing and lay down on the bed. His thoughts stayed on her before he closed his eyes. Her quiet pleasantness was deceptive. Behind that first impression was an undoubtedly brilliant young woman. Maybe there was a little girl behind the dedicated botanist. Designers were fond of saying form should follow function. Nature had been doing that for millennia. The design of every flower, plant, tree, and rock fitted its function. But sometimes nature disguised function with form, played its own tricks. Were there two Linda Corrigans, he wondered, or one simply in disguise? He let the smile stay with him as sleep came and the night grew still.

He didn't know how long he'd slept, at least a few hours, when his wild-creature hearing set him awake. He sat up, listened, heard the sounds, shuffling footsteps, a muffled cry. He swung long legs from the bed, pulled on trousers and gun belt, and swung the cabin door open. The sounds were suddenly less muffled, a man's voice. "Where is he, goddammit?" the questioner, rasped, followed by the sound of a slap and Linda's short cry of pain. "You got him here, dammit."

"No," Linda said.

Fargo went into the night, crouched, and started for the house. "Look in that other cabin," a man said, and Fargo recognized the voice of the man with the bristly mustache. Dropping to one knee, Fargo raised the Colt, then lowered it. He could bring them down easily as they charged toward the cabin, but that would leave the others holding Linda. They'd not hesitate to kill her, he knew. He backed quickly into the deepest shadows at the rear of the small cabin as the door of the house opened and the two figures charged out.

They headed for the cabin, and Fargo cursed softly. They'd see clothes and the rumpled bed, assume Kenny had run out. They'd shout the alarm to the house. It could be enough for the others to shoot Linda. Fargo cursed again. He had to take out the two men and do it silently. The throwing knife lay in its calf holster under the bed, and he swore as he stayed on one knee, let his hand grope along the ground. The two men reached the cabin door as his hand suddenly halted, his fingers touching something smooth, hard, and curved. A rock, he thought at first, then ran his fingers across the object, frowned as he felt it taper outward at the top. He closed his hand around it, lifted, and saw it was one of Linda's clay pots. It would have to do, he thought. Perhaps it was only fitting. The two men charged into the cabin and he laid the Colt on the ground beside his knee. He'd have to move with split-second timing and absolute accuracy, he knew.

Gathering his muscles, nerves and the combination of all the senses called marksmanship, he waited, his arm upraised, the clay pot clutched in his hand. The two men raced from the cabin in seconds, starting toward the house. But the clay pot was already hurtling through the air, its smooth, curved contours offering almost no wind friction. Fargo saw it smash into the first of the two men before he'd taken three steps from the doorway, smashing into pieces as it struck. The man collapsed on the spot as though his legs had suddenly evaporated, and he crumpled to the ground. The other man turned to stare at him in surprise, frowning, taking precious seconds to comprehend what had happened. When he finally tore his eyes away from the crumpled figure, he looked up, but the Colt was whistling toward him. He saw it too late as it materialized out of the darkness, hurtling end over end. The butt smashed into his forehead and Fargo hear a faint cracking sound.

The man staggered and collapsed, hitting the ground only seconds before Fargo reached him. Scooping up the Colt, Fargo started for the house, but halted as the voice came. "What's taking Jake and Benny so goddamn long?" it asked.

"Something's wrong," the mustached man snarled. Fargo heard him drag Linda with him as he made for the door. Flattening himself on the ground, Fargo rolled almost to the trees, then stayed on the ground, but with a better view of the doorway. The two men emerged together, both with revolvers raised. The mustached one had one arm around Linda's neck, the gun held to her head. "One shot and she's dead," he shouted. Fargo swore under his breath. He couldn't risk a shot in the half-light from the doorway. Even if he hit his target, the man's finger would pull the trigger in a reflex action. Fargo lay silently as the two men moved together across the open ground toward the horses a dozen feet away. Both were nervous, he knew, both peering into the night as they pushed Linda to the horses with them.

They'd take her with them, and it'd be at least a minute before he could get to the Ovaro in the stable. They might hang onto her as a hostage or discard her with a bullet. Either way she faced certain death. Fargo rose to a crouch. He knew they'd not pick him out against the blackness of the trees. He moved with the two figures, step by shuffling step, stayed abreast of them as they neared the horses. There'd be a few precious seconds when one pushed Linda onto the horse. He'd have to pull the gun from her head to get her into the saddle.

Fargo was directly opposite the two men as they reached the horses, the Colt raised in his hand. The mustached one with Linda pushed her against his horse. He reached down and grabbed her by one leg, half lifted and half threw her up into the saddle. But his gun was not against her temple. The vital seconds were there. Fargo fired the Colt, a single shot. The mustached man whirled, fell backward against his horse, and stayed there until the animal bolted. He slid to the ground in a heap, and Fargo saw Linda leap from the saddle and hit the ground on her hands and knees. He also saw the last man astride his horse, sending the animal racing into the darkness.

Fargo ran past Linda as she pushed herself up and leaped on the other horse. "No loose ends," he tossed at her as he spurred the horse forward. He picked up the fleeing rider at once, the man racing down the twisting wagon path. Fargo wished he was riding the Ovaro as the horse plodded after the other animal. But the fleeing rider was trying too hard, his horse taking the curves too wide, the animal overstriding as the man pushed it instead of collecting its motion. Fargo saw he was gaining, drew closer, and waited for the next twisting curve to appear. When it did, the fleeing rider flew around it, presenting himself sideways for an instant. It was enough. Fargo fired and saw the man sail from the horse, smashing onto the ground in a tangle of arms and legs, then lying still.

Fargo walked the horse to the figure, peered down at it for another moment, then turned the horse and rode back to the house. As he approached, he saw Linda in the doorway, the revolver in her hand. She ran toward him as she recognized him, and he swung to the ground in time to catch her as she flung herself against him, arms wrapped around his neck. She clung to him as a wet leaf clings to a rock and he felt the small points press into his chest with firm roundness.

"I never thought they'd come up here looking," she said.

"They must want Kenny very badly," Fargo said. "There has to be a reason. What did he have, or what did he know?" She shrugged helplessly and stepped back, her eyes wide. "I think you'd best find out, for your own protection."

"I will, I will," Linda said.

"This much is over," he said reassuringly.

"Stay with me, Fargo. I don't want to be alone," she said.

"Sure thing," he said and her hand curled around his. She led him into the adjoining room, where he saw the large bed fluffed with pillows. Her hand was still holding his as she reached the bed and pulled him onto it with her. Her eyes roamed across his face, down to his chest as he felt her hands tugging at his gun belt, then his trousers. He shed both and watched as, on both knees, she faced him, lifted the short nightgown, and tossed it over her head.

He felt the sharp intake of breath and the rush of surprise that swept through him. He felt not unlike a collector who'd come upon a gem of unexpected beauty, a small but totally entrancing find. She stayed very straight and very still, showing herself for him, enjoying the appreciation in his eyes. He savored the moment. It was worth savoring. The small breasts fit perfectly with the rest of her, and they thrust upward with insouciance, almost impudence. Each sharp little pink nipple seemed to reach from its soft pink circle, and below her breasts a lean chest and narrow waist curved beautifully down to narrow hips and a flat, almost concave little belly.

Just below that a small triangle rose up, almost devoid of anything but a soft fuzz, yet entirely in keeping with the rest of her. He took in legs that were lean yet not without lovely lines, thighs filling out where they touched each other. The little-girl look clung to her, he noted, but now it melded with a simmering womanliness. He reached out. It was time to stop looking. It was time to find out about contrasts.